IN any event, I am here in your room and for whatever reason, we are compromised. It is my fault entirely, Miss Alcott," said Lord Arundale.

Before Drina could question him further there came a scream and she looked up; the young Earl looked around and there stood Lady Lythe in the doorway. Behind her loomed the bulk of Sir Arthur, whose face was brick red.

"Arundale! I'll have your hide for this, you scoundrel!"

The young man got quickly to his feet. "Sir Arthur," he began, but he was not allowed to continue.

Lady Lythe stormed into the room, glaring at her niece. "You brazen hussy! How dare you cause this scandal?"

"Aunt Constance . . ."

"There will be no scandal, Lady Lythe," the Earl said in an authoritative voice, "so please be so good as to stay silent and no one but the five of us will know of it."

"That is all very well, Arundale," Sir Arthur began, "but my niece's reputation . . ."

He began to move towards the door. "No one will care a fig about her reputation when she becomes my wife, sir."

Fawcett Crest Books
by Rachelle Edwards:

DEVIL'S BRIDE
A HASTY MARRIAGE
RECKLESS MASQUERADE
THE THIEF OF HEARTS

A
HASTY
MARRIAGE

Rachelle Edwards

FAWCETT CREST • NEW YORK

A HASTY MARRIAGE

THIS BOOK CONTAINS THE COMPLETE TEXT
OF THE ORIGINAL HARDCOVER EDITION.

Published by Fawcett Crest Books, a unit of CBS
Publications, the Consumer Publishing Division of CBS Inc.,
by arrangement with Robert Hale & Company

ISBN: 0-449-23694-3

Printed in the United States of America

10 9 8 7 6 5 4 3 2 1

A
HASTY
MARRIAGE

ONE

DRINA thought it must be very late, for there had long ceased to be noises in the house and now there was only the occasional sound of a carriage being driven recklessly along The Steyne. Yet, despite the fatigue of her own mind and body, she could not sleep, and as she lay there wakeful, staring into the dark, a chink of light appeared in front of her.

"Drina," came a whisper. "Drina, are you awake?"

She was tempted not to reply, to feign sleep, for on this occasion she felt like nothing less than one of her cousin's customary midnight tête-à-têtes, even though midnight had passed many hours ago and they were well into the new day. Instead of diminishing, the chink of light grew wider and Drina could see Louisa, clad in her nightgown, clutching a candle which flickered in the draught of the open doorway. Drina eased herself into a half-sitting position.

"Louisa, you should be asleep by now," she whispered.

Her cousin giggled. "So should you." She quickly crossed the room and placed the candle on the bedside. "Oh, Drina, I couldn't possibly sleep tonight. I am far too excited. Isn't it all wonderful?"

Drina gazed at her cousin in the half-light. The girl's blonde curls were escaping her night-cap and her blue eyes were wide and dark.

"What do you mean?"

Louisa climbed on to the bed and gripped her cousin's hands. "Silly goose. I mean everything is wonderful, and especially now that Harborough has invited us all to stay at Southways! What could be more exciting than that? Mama says he is sure to offer for me once we are there. Do *you* think he will, Drina?"

The older girl smiled in the darkness. "I believe it is very likely. He seems exceedingly fond of you."

Louisa hugged herself. "Only fancy, Drina! Piers is heir to the Earl of Southway."

"Piers?"

The girl blushed. "Lord Harborough, I mean."

10

Immediately she recovered her momentary embarrassment. "I shall be a countess one day. The Countess of Southway. That is, if he does offer for me," she added quickly.

Drina continued to watch her indulgently. "I don't think there is any doubt of it, and when you are a countess I hope you will remember your cousin and still be kind to her."

"You are a silly! As if I could forget *you*. I'd as lief forget Mama and Papa. Besides, you will be married too by then and we shall visit each other and bring our children also." She laughed delightedly at the notion and did not notice in the darkness the shadow which crossed her cousin's face. "Oh, here am I making plans for us and there is no certainty that Pie . . . Harborough will offer for me at all."

"I assume that Uncle Arthur approves if Harborough does make an offer next week."

Louisa sighed. "Father says Viscount Harborough is an eminently suitable match. Besides," she added in a more matter-of-fact tone, "Father is ready to go home to Rington Manor. He says he cannot face another London Season, although Mama, as you know, is enjoying every moment of it. Even if Harborough does offer for me, we shall not be married until at least the spring, so there is still a great deal of fun ahead of us. What have you enjoyed most about London, Drina?"

The older girl sighed. "That, Louisa, is a very difficult question. I have enjoyed everything so much."

"Meeting the Regent?" Louisa suggested with a laugh. "He's so fat, but so sweet I cannot help but like him."

"I did not meet him."

The girl looked abashed. "I forgot! I cannot conceive why your name was not included in the invitation. It was a dreadful oversight. The Pavilion, Drina, is so magnificent. I wish you could have seen it. The Duchess of Portchester says Prinny wanted it to be like an Eastern harem!"

Drina laughed. "I did enjoy Mrs Siddon's at-home when she recited Shakespeare, but I have loved every moment in London. After all, we have lived so quietly at Rington Manor."

"That is true. I don't know how Mama and Papa could bear it all those years. Did you know what Mr Hitchin said to me tonight, Drina?"

"Tell me," she urged, warming once again to her cousin's spontaneous gaiety.

"He said he had never seen anyone who suited blue so well!"

Drina did not doubt the sincerity of that sentiment. Louisa was indeed lovely, and since her introduction into Society she had taken the *ton* by storm. Several offers of marriage had been made but none until now had been deemed suitable.

"His wife's nose positively quivered with anger," she went on happily. "Of course, everyone knows he married her only for her fortune. I would hate to be married for *my* portion. You don't think Harborough is interested in *that*, do you?"

Drina's laugh rang out. "Now who is the goose? I am quite certain there is nothing further from his mind. Half the beaux in London have been in love with you this Season. Lord Harborough has had eyes for no one else for weeks, and you know it!"

"I'm sure he was jealous when Lord Arundale gave me his arm into supper tonight. I saw him speak to you earlier. Did he say anything about me?"

"Who? Lord Harborough?"

Louisa laughed. "No! Lord Arundale."

Louisa was unable to see the dull flush that had spread up her cousin's cheeks. "Nothing. He merely procured some lemonade for me also when Aunt Constance mentioned a thirst."

"He was very attentive during supper. Everyone was most surprised."

Drina struggled out of the enveloping folds of the feather pillows. "Louisa, perhaps he is in love with you too. Would you not prefer . . . ?"

The girl covered her lips with her fingers to suppress a giggle. "Harborough will suit me well enough, even though Arundale is just about the richest man in all England."

"He is extremely handsome too," Drina added wistfully, recalling with great clarity the moment when he had handed her the lemonade and had smiled at her. At that moment she had felt as though she were the most beautiful girl in the world, although in fact he had probably not even noticed her.

"I find him rather daunting," her cousin replied. "I could never be *comfortable* in his company. Besides, Amy Vincent told me—on the night of Lady Furstlove's rout—that Lord Arundale had his heart broken by a beauty who ran away with another man years ago. Since then he has devoted his life to the breeding and training of horses and has never been seriously interested in any woman."

"I cannot imagine any woman preferring another to Lord Arundale," Drina said wistfully.

There was a brief silence between the two, and then Louisa clapped her hands together. "Drina! I do believe you are partial to the Earl. How strange. I would never have thought it of you."

Drina turned her head away. "Nonsense! You are imagining things. How could I be partial to him! I have scarce exchanged a word with him, and who am I to have a partiality to the Earl of Arundale?"

Impulsively, Louisa caught her cousin's hands in hers. "Oh, Drina, my love, how I wish you were getting married too. It would be so much fun to be making plans together."

"One day . . ."

"No, *now*, and to one of the gentlemen we have met in London."

Drina sank back into the pillows once more. "For that I should require either looks or fortune, Louisa, and I am only too well aware I have neither."

"Oh, Drina," her cousin moaned. "That is not true. You are very handsome, and if all those fortune-hunters cannot see it then it is a grievous loss to them!"

The older girl smiled reassuringly at her cousin. "Do not concern yourself about me, my dear. I am very fortunate to have so congenial a home and such kind relatives."

"You should have had a Season too by rights. I told Mama so at the time, but she said there wasn't enough money to launch both of us."

"That is perfectly true, Louisa."

"She said that your Mama had a Season, and precious little good it did her too . . ."

"Louisa," Drina said firmly, "I would not have wanted a Season, I assure you. I would have found it very difficult; I cannot socialise as easily as you."

"But it *is* easy. When I am married I shall make sure you meet the right young men."

15

Her cousin laughed. "They are hardly likely to be interested."

Louisa frowned. "Drina, did you really not want to marry Mr Kingsby last year?"

Her heart sank at the reminder of her uncle's neighbour who had offered for her so unexpectedly a year ago. Mr Kingsby was an influential man in the neighbourhood who rode to hounds with Sir Arthur Lythe, a lifelong friend in fact. He owned a considerable parcel of land and a house almost as handsome as Rington Manor, but he was at least fifty years old, a widower with five grown-up children for whom Drina had no regard either. They were all disagreeable creatures who for years had constantly teased Drina for her position in her uncle's household.

At Drina's refusal Lady Lythe had been furious, but Drina was adamant. One look at Mr Kingsby's corpulence, his florid face, and those small eyes which looked upon her so lecherously, she knew she would rather die than marry him, and resolved to do so.

"I made my decision a year ago and have never regretted it," she answered after a moment or two, and then, swinging her legs over the side of the bed, she added, "You must go back to your room, Louisa, or you will not get any sleep tonight and it would not do to go to Southways with dark shadows beneath your eyes."

Louisa laughed. "Oh, you sound like Mama now, but you are always right, Drina, and so sensible. Do you recall our childhood days when I was afraid of the dark and always came into your bed?"

"Yes, I recall it well," she replied, gazing fondly at her cousin. After a moment she picked up the candle and handed it to her. "Sleep well, Louisa." She bent and kissed her forehead.

"Good night, Drina. I hope your dreams will be as sweet as mine."

When she had gone, closing the door behind her Drina sighed. She went to the window and pulled aside the heavy brocade curtain, gazing out at the stillness of the sea. It looked so beautiful, silvered by the light of the moon. And it was all so calm, so different from the hustle and bustle of the daytime when the sea was crowded with bathing machines and boats, and The Steyne was made a dangerous place to stroll by bucks racing their curricles to show off the superiority of their experience and expensive horseflesh.

After a few minutes she allowed the curtain to drop and wandered disconsolately towards the dressing-table. She sank down on to the stool, gazing at her own murky reflection in the mirror. She wondered why she felt so dispirited and could only assume it was because at last Louisa was about to be married.

She would miss her bright presence, and that was the root of her unease. Darling, lively Louisa and her constant pursuit of fun and pleasure. She had been a joy to Drina ever since she went to live at Rington Manor after the death of her own father. A mere three years separated them in age, but it seemed more like ten, such was their relationship. Drina had enjoyed Louisa's Season even though her own role forced her into the background. Up until then, to tell the truth, country life at Rington Manor at the mercy of Aunt Constance's uncertain moods had often bored and depressed her, even though any alternative to such a life did not bear thinking about. Lady Constance Lythe had not taken her orphaned niece to her heart even though her husband had insisted they take her into their home. No one was more aware of this than Drina. At Rington Manor the quiet tenor of life, the card parties interspersed with fox hunts and shooting parties, had not suited her temperament, which was strange, for she had known little else. And she obeyed her aunt's every command dutifully, although she did, at times, resent the unfairness of Lady Lythe's attitude to her.

What I wouldn't give to be one of the hostesses of the *ton*, she thought. I would make more glittering occasions than any of them had ever seen before.

She wound a strand of hair around her finger.

It was much too dark and heavy—not at all fashionable—and her eyes were dark too, considered far too direct and bold for her aunt's taste. But just for one moment last night. . . .

She turned away from the mirror. It wouldn't do to think about such matters, or men like the Earl of Arundale who were polite to her out of consideration for Lady Lythe and Louisa. She must instead steel herself for a return to the sterile life at Rington Manor with memories of so many exciting happenings during Louisa's one brief London Season.

Oh, how she had enjoyed it all! The operas and plays, the balls, the routs and card parties. It had all been made so much more enjoyable by the recent defeat of Bonaparte after so many years of war, and this had been followed by magnificent tableaux and firework displays to mark the ending of fighting with France. Here in Brighton they had even seen a French touring company enact plays unseen in England for a generation.

Drina snuggled down into the bed once more. Sleep was never further away. Louisa deserved a happy marriage and Harborough would care for her well, but she could not suppress a twinge of envy, wishing she too could look forward to such felicity with a man so much in love with her. She was not, it was true, so ill-looking, and surely fortune was not of importance to all men. Her own father did not look for one. She sighed again. That was, she realised, the reason she was forced to depend on her uncle's charity. To one with such spirit as Drina Alcott it became her ill.

The streets of Brighton were almost deserted when the Earl of Arundale came out of the Marine Pavilion, dismissed his carriage and decided on such a pleasant morning to stroll back to the house which he had rented for the summer. He passed a couple of beaux who aspired to the fashionable world at present assembled at Brighton where the Prince Regent was holding Court, and they were indeed fashionably attired, although exceedingly drunk, teasing the link boy who lighted their way.

As they staggered past, one of the bucks raised a hand and called, "Good morning to you, My Lord Arundale!"

Pausing to look at them, his lordship recognised that one of the men was a Captain Hugo Lythe, the son of Sir Arthur Lythe and his pretentious wife.

"Time you were abed, Lythe," the Earl answered, and the young man merely laughed.

"How's Prinny this morning?" shouted the one the Earl did not recognise as they staggered away, still laughing.

Impudent puppies, he thought, but he

reached his house with no further interruption, waking his footman on entry.

"Sir Francis Petley to see you, my lord," the man said as he suppressed a yawn and received his master's cane, evening cape and hat.

The Earl was taken aback. "At this time of the morning?"

"Yes, my lord. He has been waiting an hour."

He bounded up the stairs and into the study where his friend was dozing in a high wing chair. "Francis! What in heaven's name is wrong?"

The young man came awake with a start. "What? Oh. Hm. You're back at last." He sat up straight in the chair and smoothed down his coat. "Didn't expect you back so late, that's the truth."

The Earl sank down on the edge of the desk. "Prinny had a fancy to talk horseflesh."

Sir Francis nodded his complete understanding of the situation and then he frowned. "He can be a blasted bore when he chooses. Did y'see the way he held Hélène's hands for a full five minutes last night?"

The Earl's eyes lit up with amusement. "You can be thankful, Francis, that today His Highness can do little more than hold a lady's hand. A few years ago you would have had good cause to worry."

The man's face relaxed. "Touchy where

m'wife's concerned, Simon, but I suppose you've noticed."

"With one as lovely as Lady Petley, you are wise to be concerned. But that isn't why you're here at this hour of the morning. Come, my friend, tell me what brings you here."

"Couldn't think of a better time when we can parley in private, Simon, and that's the truth."

"Parley about what?" his friend asked with interest.

"You are going to Southways next week. . . ."

The Earl drew a sigh. "Truth to tell, Francis, I had thought of crying off that particular engagement."

"Oh, surely not? Harborough will put on a good show."

"You and I know it's only an excuse to see the Lythe chit in his home background."

"The man's besotted."

"Quite. Well, she's a pretty enough little thing in an insipid way, and she has a respectable portion. I dare say she will do."

"Insipid or not, it would take a great deal to 'do' for you these days, Simon," his friend retorted. "But I must say, I did think for a while that you might . . ."

The Earl laughed harshly. "You didn't really, Francis? Surely you know me better than that after all these years."

"At least I hoped."

He laughed again. "Louisa Lythe! Well, that

really beats the Dutch." His friend looked discomforted. "What is more, neither have I a fancy to watch Harborough do his wooing."

"Oh, come now. By all accounts it'll be a large houseparty. Don't cry off, Simon. It's what I've come to talk about with you." He looked away again. "I want you to keep an eye on m'wife for me while you're there."

The Earl stared at him in astonishment for a moment or two and then said in a quiet voice, "Why can't you do that for yourself?"

"Because I've been recalled to London next week. Hélène refuses to come with me; says she's been looking forward to Southways too much. Can't say I blame her either. It's dev'lish dull in London just now."

"What can be so urgent now?" the Earl asked, immediately diverted from so strange a request. "No trouble with the Congress?"

"No more than usual. More parties than discussions in Vienna, so I'm told. This business is something else, Simon. We've had some disturbing reports from our agents in Paris . . ."

The Earl went to sit in a chair, facing his friend. "Agents? Surely all that has finished now Boney's on Elba."

His friend smiled grimly. "We hope so, but there is still plenty of intrigue going on and we know that Boney's agents are still active. The Minister's just had a report that an important agent is now in England. It is believed in diplomatic circles that Boney's far from finished, or at least he hopes to be."

The Earl drew a deep sigh. "The Devil take him.

"And why," he asked moments later, "do you wish anyone to keep an eye on Lady Petley?"

Sir Francis took a pinch of snuff. "God knows it's difficult to put into words, and to you of all people, but you're the only one I *can* ask."

The Earl gazed across at him with a merciless stare which Sir Francis was unable to hold. He turned away.

"I just want an eye keeping on her. You know the way I feel about her . . ."

The Earl sighed again. "Yes."

"She's been acting rather strangely of late, Simon. Furtive is the only way I can describe it. Yesterday I caught her burning some paper."

"I see."

"I am not sure that I do. I'm wretched, Simon. Jealous, suspicious. If only I didn't adore her so."

"Your wife's behaviour is always exemplary."

"I know that! She barely flirts in public, despite all the temptations. But I know so . . ."

". . . so little of her," his friend finished in a quiet voice.

Sir Francis hung his head. "Of course you do right to remind me of the haste in which we were wed and how you advised me against it at the time."

"I shall do nothing of the kind."

"If only you knew how much I love her you would understand . . ."

The Earl stood up and went to a table on which stood an array of cut-glass decanters. "Oh, God! I've caught you on the raw there, all right," Sir Francis gasped, looking at his friend in horror.

"Have a brandy, Francis."

"No, no. I've had too much already. Too much of a blabberer; that's my trouble. I shouldn't have said that to you, Simon. I'm sorry."

The Earl kept his back on his friend as he raised his glass to his lips. "I think you and I have been friends long enough not to need to apologise to one another."

His friend looked considerably relieved but nonetheless concerned. "I recall very clearly a time when you spoke to me very firmly," the Earl went on.

Sir Francis laughed unevenly. "You were roaring drunk at the time and you wanted to fight me for even trying to talk sense to you. You threatened to knock my head off."

"What a fool I was—all because of a woman. I can scarce recall that emotion now."

"*I* was a fool to speak to you about something I knew nothing about."

"At least this is about the woman to whom you are married."

"It's the doubts and suspicions which make me like this, Simon."

The Earl turned to face him once again. "You are wise not to ignore them as I did with Fenella." There was a silence between them, and then the Earl added, "I am convinced you are wrong about this. There must be some other explanation to her behaviour."

"You really believe that, despite the fact that you were against our marrying?"

"I merely advised caution."

Sir Francis laid his head back on the chair. "Caution. How could I wait? She was so lovely, so alone, so wretched, and I had to return to London within the se'night. I never told you how we met, did I?"

"Not the precise circumstances."

"That was possibly because I knew you would disapprove even more strongly, and I was in no mind to be talked out of it. We were all mad in Paris this year. It was victory, and everyone welcomed us. Women were eager—oh, you know how it is, Simon. Everyone was anxious to embrace the victors. Even though I was there on diplomatic business, it was more like one long party.

"Then, early one morning, as I was walking back to the hotel along the banks of the Seine, I saw this creature about to fling herself in. It was a common enough occurrence in Paris at that time, but I had never witnessed it before. I caught her in my arms before she could fall. Hélène. Oh, I am sure I fell in love with her at that very moment. She looked so pitiful and yet so lovely. I put her into the care of the Marchioness of Flaverton who took her under her wing. The girl was so grateful."

He sat up. "She looked like a vagabond when I first set eyes on her, but she is an aristocrat; a member of the Duc de Cabouchard's family. Many of them perished during the Terror, but Hélène's parents escaped disguised as peasants. They were forced into menial work to survive, as was my poor Hélène when she grew older. She fell in love, eventually, with a corporal in Boney's army and it seemed her future would be happier, until he was killed just before the fall of Paris. How she hates that Corsican upstart! Up until that despairing moment when she contemplated death, she was alone and unprotected in a Paris overrun by foreign soldiers.

"Heaven knows I've liked the ladies, but since I married Hélène I've never so much as looked at another, and we have been happy, Simon."

He buried his head in his hands. For a long moment his friend gazed at him. Lady Hélène Petley had behaved impeccably at all times in his presence, but it still remained that the Earl could not rid himself of the suspicion that she was a calculating young woman and not all she should be. But it was only a feeling, and he didn't doubt that she had made his friend happy.

After a moment the Earl laid his hand on his friend's shoulder. "And so you shall be in the future. But do not ask me to spy on her."

At this the young man jumped to his feet. "I did not ask you to!" And then his angry gaze fell away. "Simon, I'm in agonies all the time. I'm afire with jealousy of any man who as much as looks at her. I could kill them all."

The Earl's gaze was pitying. "You must control such a fever, my friend, or it will destroy you."

Sir Francis looked at him appealingly. "When . . . Fenella left you, did you not want to . . . kill the man who had taken her from you? I was so sure you would challenge him to a duel. You must have felt . . . you must have wanted . . ."

The Earl stared ahead of him, past his friend. "Yes, I was gripped by a feeling of violence. The feeling, for a while, was overwhelming, but I never thought of challenging that fellow to a duel; after all, I could not blame him, for I loved her to distraction myself. I just wanted to kill all females. I wanted to put my hands around their white throats and squeeze the life out of them." He glanced at Sir Francis and smiled at his astonishment. "There, that is the first time I have spoken of it even to you."

"Do you still feel so intense a hatred?"

"It passed, and I decided four-legged fillies would be more true to me, and so I devote my time to them."

"But, Simon, there have been women in your life since then, surely."

He smiled again, but it was an empty one. He put his glass down on the desk. "Many of them, but not of our own kind, Francis. None of them are ladies with whom I had to be chaperoned, to whom I would have to give my name before I could so much as kiss their treacherous lips. Since Fenella left me I've known many females, Francis, all of them inadmissible to the drawing-rooms of our acquaintances, but a good deal truer. They don't demand my name or my fortune, or even devotion. It suits me far better than the agonies of the so-called love of equals."

"Then I can scarce expect understanding from you if your feelings are so hardened."

"Oh, I do understand," he answered in a gentle voice.

"But you will not help me."

"The thought is totally abhorrent to me."

Sir Francis gripped his sleeve. "I beg of you, Simon, help to end this torment. I keep wondering if she is to see her lover at Southways next week and if that is the reason she is so anxious to go there without me."

The Earl laughed. "It is your imagination and nothing more, believe me."

Sir Francis stood back and the Earl smoothed out the wrinkles from his sleeve. "This from you who has cause to believe no woman can be faithful."

"I never said that, Francis. Many females have a true heart, I don't doubt. And as far as Lady Petley is concerned I have rarely seen any woman take such an interest in her husband or his affairs."

"That is true," Sir Francis admitted, but there was no brightening of his manner.

The Earl put his hand on his friend's shoulder again. "Francis, if I were to . . . observe Lady Petley in company. . . . Only observe her, mind you. . . ."

The other man immediately brightened. "Would you? I would be so grateful, Simon."

"Would you believe me if I were to report on her complete innocence?"

Sir Francis gazed at him for a moment or two and then clasped him about the shoulders. "I trust you, my friend."

He sighed. "So be it. Now go on back to your bride or she will be fully justified in seeking attention elsewhere."

The other man smiled for the first time. "You

are a true friend, Simon. I knew I could rely on you."

As he hurried out of the room the Earl shook his head, pitying anyone so much in love. He had travelled that road himself and could testify that such folly only led to grief.

TWO

It was, as Sir Francis Petley had predicted, a large houseparty at Southways. The company, however, was far from brilliant and, filled with distaste by the task set him, the Earl of Arundale could not be said to be enjoying himself. True, the fishing at the Earl of Southway's estate was good, but the shooting was indifferent and the bag far from satisfactory to so good a shot as the Earl of Arundale. The evenings passed pleasantly enough, although the Earl was not moved by the musical accomplishments of those young ladies brought forward to sing or to play a tune on the pianoforte. Neither could he be enthusiastic about the charades being enacted by the younger members of the party.

As he sat in the high-ceilinged drawing-room of Southways he feigned an interest in all around him and even he had to admit that Lady Petley had a sweet voice and played well the French traditional tunes with which she was captivating her audience.

For the first time since her marriage to his friend, the Earl studied her objectively, and had his heart not been turned to ice so long ago it would have been possible for him to admit her a desirable woman, every man's dream of beauty. Her skin was the translucent white which only served to heighten the red of her hair, and her eyes were as green as the Petley emeralds which glittered around her neck. Tonight, Captain Hugo Lythe was favoured to turn her music, but on previous evenings there had been others and at all times her behaviour had been perfectly proper. He could not fault Hélène Petley. He did not doubt her antecedents were aristocratic—such breeding was in every fibre of her being—and she had proved the perfect hostess for Sir Francis, only the Earl wished Hélène were married to someone other than his dear friend. At the back of his mind there remained a nagging doubt.

"She is a gracious woman, is she not?" came a voice close to his ear.

The Earl turned to find at his side a gentleman he had been introduced to as a Mr Augustus Fine, someone he was coming across with increased frequency at gatherings such as this.

The Earl glared at Mr Fine, angry at being caught out observing Lady Petley with such intensity, and so he managed only to murmur a reply, hoping that the man would go away.

But Mr Fine made no move to go away. As Lady Petley was prevailed upon to continue her recital the man said, "My lord, I am informed that you are some expert on horseflesh. . . ."

"I do not admit to it," he answered irritably. "It is others who accredit me with such knowledge."

"Come, come now, you underestimate yourself, my lord. Everyone knows you own one of the finest studs in the country and employ the best trainer at your stables."

The Earl acknowledged the compliment, and the man went on, "I am hoping to purchase my own racehorse in the near future. Perhaps you would be kind enough . . ."

"You require my advice?"

"I beg it, my lord. I am fond of the turf, but know little enough of the technicalities, and I do wish for a superior animal. The best possible."

The Earl stared at the man for a moment or two. He was of small stature but powerfully built; the Earl judged him to be approaching fifty years, and he was fashionably yet tastefully attired. It was probable he was a newcomer to the *haut ton*, possibly having acquired a fortune either by inheritance or by trade, although it was difficult to judge. Clearly everyone found his presence in their homes acceptable, hence his frequent appearances in elevated company.

"I would advise you to buy at Tattersall's, sir. There you are certain to find an animal to your liking and one which suits your purse."

"Do you not have any in your stables, my lord? I am told one cannot find any better."

"I am flattered, but I rarely sell, Mr Fine. All my efforts are to acquire horses. However, if you are in earnest about buying a superior animal and you wish to avail yourself of my trainer, I would be glad . . ."

The man looked delighted. "I am *most* obliged."

The Earl was glad to have caused so much happiness and was forced to smile. "I spend a great deal of time on my Suffolk estates amongst the horses. The next time I travel down you must take the opportunity of visiting me and inspecting the stables."

"It would be a great pleasure!"

The Earl was surprised at his own generosity, but somehow, so engaging was his manner, he could not consider this man an upstart. Lady Petley had finished her recital and was being applauded by the assembled guests. The Earl and Mr Fine joined in, and then the younger man got to his feet as the Countess of Southway announced supper.

"You will excuse me, Mr Fine?"

He went across the room to where Lady Petley was still standing on the dais by the pianoforte. The Earl offered her his arm. "Allow me to escort you, Lady Petley."

The woman beamed at so unexpected an invitation and several other gentlemen in attendance scowled at him. "Why, Lord Arundale, what a pleasure." She linked her arm into his and they made their way into the supper-room. "I noticed," she went on in that very attractive accent of hers, "you had the largest catch of all when you returned from fishing today."

"I was very satisfied."

He found a quiet corner in which she could sit and he then brought the food to her a few moments later.

"I have seen so little of you since we arrived, Lord Arundale," she told him.

"It is difficult to break through the ring of admirers who are always around you."

She laughed. "It is no compensation, alas, for the absence of my dear Francis."

"It is unfortunate that business keeps him in London this week."

"I was never more surprised, for I truly believed that once the terrible Bonaparte was exiled I would be able to see more of my husband."

"There will always be matters of the utmost importance for those connected with the Foreign Ministry."

"So I discover, and it is too bad." She began to enjoy the cold collation, and after a moment asked, "Lord Arundale, do you happen to know what this particular matter is about?"

The Earl paused in his eating to gaze at her, and then answered, "I really cannot say."

Lady Petley sighed again. "I have nightmares about it all happening again, you know."

"I can appreciate your fears; however, I don't think you need worry, Lady Petley."

She smiled tremulously. "You are very kind to reassure me, Lord Arundale. It is only that I fear for all I have—Francis, and this wonderful country where I have found peace. Francis does reassure me constantly, but he is not always allowed to discuss Ministry matters with me, and when he is called to meetings with Lord Castlereagh I fear something is afoot."

"Francis would not reassure you if there was no cause."

Her lips trembled again. "I am sure you are right. Oh, look, there is the delightful Miss Lythe with Lord Harborough. Do you think he will announce their engagement soon?"

"It is very possible, if the gossips are to be believed."

"And there is Miss Alcott, the companion, I think. How very sad to be in such a position. I cannot help but be thankful I escaped such a fate. Do you find honesty distasteful, Lord Arundale?"

He swallowed a mouthful of ham he had been chewing and gazed at her once more. "Not at all, Lady Petley," he answered after a moment or two. "I find it distinctly refreshing."

She smiled at him, and he could understand so well his friend's feelings. This woman could so easily bewitch a man; he, himself, was responding to her charm in a way impossible for more than ten years.

Drina Alcott was standing by the supper table, oblivious to the milling throng about her. She had been watching Lord Arundale and the captivating Lady Petley for some few minutes. They were in earnest conversation and were not aware of her observation of them. She couldn't help but notice how well they looked together. The Earl's dark, brooding looks contrasted so well with the fragility of the woman at his side.

A moment later Louisa came hurrying up to her. She was wearing a white gauze dress embroidered with seed pearls and as she hurried up to her cousin Drina thought she looked rather like a butterfly. Her own dress was somewhat plainer and a shade of pink which did not become her, but her aunt would hear no argument against it, so pink it had been.

"I was wondering where you had got to!" Drina exclaimed.

"I met the Duchess of Saltbury on my way in and I couldn't get away. Mama is still talking to her, although how I don't know. She can only hear through that ear trumpet of hers and one has to shout very loudly."

They both laughed. "Come and have some supper," Drina urged. "There is your favourite lobster mousse and the ham is delicious. I am afraid I've eaten far too much and will not be able to sleep."

"I couldn't eat a thing!" She gripped Drina's hands tightly in her own. "Oh, Drina, guess what has happened?"

"I couldn't."

"Piers and Father have gone into the library—to talk!"

"How marvellous! I'm so glad for you, my love."

"But I'm so afraid, Drina. One day I shall be mistress of all this, and the thought terrifies me!"

"You will be more than equal to it. You must have impressed him and his parents for him to offer for you. Think no more about it."

Her eyes gleamed with excitement. "It's like a whole new world opening up before me,

Drina! A secret world. Oh, my legs feel as weak as that blancmange on the table over there."

Most of the other guests were wandering back into the drawing-room where dancing would soon begin. Servants were setting up card tables so that those wishing to play could do so. The Earl had no taste for dancing, and yet playing whist for the cheeseparing stakes which were customary at Southways was not to his liking either. He preferred by far the gambling rooms at Crockford's or White's, or any of the St James's clubs that he frequented. And, of course, there were houses situated in and around the Strand where the evening's entertainment was nowhere near as genteel as in the homes of his fellow aristocrats, but far more enjoyable.

Lady Petley had long since been relinquished to several of her admirers and the Earl was wondering when he could decently excuse himself from the party and return to London to more congenial pursuits when an acquaintance of his sauntered towards him.

"Looks as though the fair Louisa is being withdrawn from circulation at last," said the Honourable James Oldham as he approached.

The Earl's eyebrows went up a fraction. "What makes you so certain, James?"

He nodded to where Sir Arthur, Viscount Harborough and the Earl of Southway were entering the room together. They appeared to be in high spirits.

"I rather think that Harborough has come up to scratch at last and that an announcement is imminent," the young man noted, not without a little malice.

"I hardly think it will be a surprise to anyone present," replied the other, who was unable to keep the boredom from creeping into his voice.

James Oldham gave him a sideways glance. "Well, this is one less for hopeful bachelors like you and me."

The Earl eyed him laconically. "Do you think so?"

"It's an ever diminishing circle."

"Not my circle, James. I find no lack of female companionship however many debutantes become engaged each Season."

The young man roared with laughter. "*Your* circle, Simon. Oh, really, what a lark! Do you know what Freddie Craven said about you at Boodle's the other month?"

"No doubt you are intent upon telling me."

"He said that when you die there will be no wife and children to follow the coffin, just a bevy of Covent Garden nuns."

"Their grief would be a great deal more genuine than that of most of the widows and children I have seen."

The other man laughed again and then became alert. "I say, Arthur Lythe looks pleased with himself, doesn't he?"

Lord Arundale drew out his snuff box and inhaled a pinch as he surveyed the gathering with a laconic eye. Then, brushing off the flecks of snuff with a lace-edged handkerchief, he moved towards the french window.

"I think," he murmured to the other man, "it is time for a turn on the terrace."

It was some considerable time later when the Earl returned to the drawing-room. The dancing had by then commenced and all the tables were occupied by those intent upon their cards. It was obvious the expected announcement had been made at last, for Viscount Harborough and his chosen bride were at the centre of a milling throng whilst near by Lady Lythe, seated on a sofa, was also at the centre of considerable attention.

Immediately he went to congratulate the prospective bridegroom, and taking Louisa's hand in his he raised it gallantly to his lips.

"Harborough is the luckiest of men," he told her, and she blushed to the roots of her hair.

The sight of Lord Harborough accepting the congratulations of his friends as if it were a God-given right, reminded him of the occasion of his own betrothal, but it was difficult now to recall the time when he too looked forward with so much confidence to a future with the woman he loved. As more people crowded

round the couple, threatening to crush his lordship, he moved away, only to be accosted by a
shrill voice.

"Ah, Lord Arundale, this is an exciting occasion, is it not?"

He glanced round at Lady Lythe and bowed
briefly to her. "Indeed it is, ma'am. May I
congratulate you on so charming a daughter?"
Lady Lythe inclined her head graciously.
"Such graciousness must," the Earl went on, enjoying himself now, "be a family trait."

Lady Lythe looked extremely gratified as she
turned to the girl sitting at her side. "Drina, I
must have left my fan in the supper-room . . ."

The girl was on her feet immediately. "I
will fetch it for you," she said in a slightly
breathless voice that was not unpleasing.

Lady Lythe smiled up at him as the girl hurried away. "Do sit down, Lord Arundale."

He hesitated and then did so. He felt sorry
for that girl, as he would anyone in such an invidious position, forced to fetch and carry and
to be at the mercy of the whims and moods of
some selfish woman. Lady Lythe, he was
certain, would not be an easy mistress, and he
recalled now that the girl had looked glum all
evening, which was not surprising either. Little
chance of marriage—any marriage—for her, let
alone one which would be so congenial. His
eyes followed her as she left the room. Pity. She

might have had quite a pleasing appearance if it were not for the appalling colour of her gown.

"Dare we hope that you may be next in line?" Lady Lythe asked coyly.

For the past fifteen years the Earl had been sickened by just such a question being asked of him, first by friends of his grandmother and then by every married woman of his acquaintance, and when he had finally acquiesced the result had been betrayal of the most humiliating kind.

"In line for what, Lady Lythe?" he asked, his eyebrows raised slightly.

She nudged him quite hard. "Marriage, of course."

He gave her a smile which betrayed nothing of his irritation. "One never knows, Lady Lythe."

"Just because my own dear Louisa is now engaged does not mean to say that there are no other handsome females who could make you as happy as my daughter has made Harborough."

"I don't doubt that is true, ma'am, only it would be a trifle difficult to find anyone to compare with Miss Lythe."

She laughed happily, and at that moment he heard a whispered voice near by say quite clearly, "Any woman *he* marries would have to walk on all fours and look like a horse not to feel out of place on that estate of his."

He glanced around and noted who had spoken. The acid tones belonged to a lady whose daughter had been pushed on to him quite forcibly on occasions during the last Season before she had become engaged to a parson. He looked at the woman coldly in a way which normally stunned most people into silence, but he did bite back a cutting reply.

The girl called Drina came hurrying back through the crowded room. She looked more unhappy than ever. "I cannot find your fan at all," she said worriedly, "and I have searched the room thoroughly and enquired of the footmen. Are you quite certain . . ."

Lady Lythe somehow managed to produce the ivory-and-lace fan from the side of her chair, laughing foolishly as she did so.

"It was here all the time! How silly of me to send you all the way for nothing, my dear."

The Earl was watching the girl and was surprised to see an unmistakable flare of anger in her eyes. In that moment she had reminded him of someone else, but as she suppressed any retort she would have liked to have made, the feeling went. Lord Arundale understood her anger all too well; Lady Lythe's behaviour was unforgivable.

Other guests were taking their partners for a country dance and suddenly the Earl got to his feet and was bowing low in front of Drina Alcott.

"Miss Alcott, may I have the pleasure of this dance if it is not already promised?"

She stared at him as if thunderstruck and he vowed he would never give way to such impulse again if she stammered and blushed at him. If not, it would be amusing. Hopefully it would brighten this poor girl's evening, it would provide him with an escape from Lady Lythe, and it would surely give the gossips something to talk about.

The girl, to his satisfaction, did not blush or stammer, for once the immediate surprise was over she straightened up and looked him directly in the eye.

"I would be delighted to dance with you, Lord Arundale," she answered firmly, and as she placed her hand on his arm he bowed to her astonished aunt and they went to take their place in the set.

THREE

Sawkins, Lord Arundale's valet, gathered up his master's clothes and, bidding him good night, left the room. As soon as the door had closed, the Earl, clad in a brocade dressing-gown embroidered with his initials and family crest, sank down into a chair and opened his book. But he could not concentrate on it, and although it was late he was used to later hours. His mind kept returning to Francis. It was true he was madly in love, beyond all reason it would appear, but was he so obsessed as to imagine his wife's duplicity? The Earl had, as promised, observed her in company and she had betrayed no particular partiality to any one person, but he realised now that if there was some liaison it would take place, not in the drawing-rooms for all to see, but in her own bedroom and late at night.

The Earl closed the book again and gazed for some time into empty space. Spying on Lady Petley was a concept totally abhorrent to him, and yet his friend's face, so full of doubts and misery, kept appearing before him. He recalled an occasion many years ago, when he had been thrown from his horse in a field and was helpless before a maddened bull. It had been Sir Francis who had risked his own life to draw off the creature whilst the Earl had a chance to run for safety. He had known Francis Petley ever since they were at Eton together, and Francis, the Earl was well aware, was not a man to give way to imagined fears and fancies.

Moments later, the Earl was opening his door and peering out into the deserted corridor where the candles in their brackets were burning low. Lady Petley's room, he knew, was situated some way from his own and he fervently hoped he would encounter no one who might misconstrue his presence in the corridors at this time of the morning. It was unlikely, for he had been up late, having been persuaded by Sir Arthur Lythe to join in a game in the billiards-room at a time when most of the other guests were making their way to bed. Of course, it was possible that some of the guests were in the habit of nocturnal visiting, but they too would take care not to be seen.

Lady Petley's room was situated at the end of the south wing. The door at the very end led to the Earl of Southway's own rooms, and to the right was Lady Petley's apartment. As he approached, careful not to make any noise on the highly polished floor, he felt not only a fool but a blackguard too. Nevertheless, he went on until he reached the door and after hesitating further he pressed his ear against it.

Some emotion he could not recognise surged through him at the sound of voices within. He could hear nothing of what was being said, but there was definitely more than one person present in the room. Suddenly he drew away, realising it could well be Lady Petley's maid attending her. He felt more foolish than ever, and angry at allowing himself to be inveigled into such madness. As he drew away he thought he heard someone inside the room cry out, but his attention had been caught by the sound of footsteps in the corridor. He whirled round and then froze, feeling more like a trapped animal than a fashionable member of the Regent's Carlton House Set.

It would be, to say the least, inconvenient to be discovered outside Lady Petley's room in his nightclothes. The footsteps continued to come closer and the Earl glanced around him, seeking any means of escape from discovery. Ahead of him was the Earl of Southway's apartments and he and his wife were definitely in them, which left only the room to his left.

The Earl reasoned that if it were unlocked it would be unoccupied, but if not the occupant would most probably be asleep by now. He tried the handle and to his great relief the door opened and he slipped inside the room just as someone came around the corner.

Drina lay awake in the four-poster bed for a long time after she had climbed into it. So, she thought, Louisa was to be married after all. It was, of course, no surprise, and had it not been Lord Harborough there would have been another beau of the *ton*, for so many of them had been in love with her since her debut into Society. After the wedding it would be back to Rington Manor for her, back to her aunt's thinly veiled tolerance of her and a life in the country which must, after London, seem more boring than ever.

Without Louisa it was bound to be miserable and she dare not venture to think that it might be for the rest of her life. Hugo, Louisa's brother lately returned from service in France with the Duke of Wellington, was no substitute. He was very much his mother's son and he too considered her a charity case, never failing to take up any opportunity to remind her of the fact, although during their childhood Drina had proved useful to him. There was no one else on whom he dare vent his cruel humour, to taunt and to pinch her, and later as she came into womanhood to kiss and fondle when he caught her alone in some dark corner. It was no use complaining either. Hugo would have deemed it quite proper to deny all allegations she might make, and his mother, of course, would have believed him.

Oh, no, the prospect of the rest of her life at Rington Manor was not a welcome one. More pleasant was to remember with pleasure that one country dance with Lord Arundale. Not that Drina was foolish enough to imagine it was anything other than an excuse to escape her aunt, who could be tiresome to others than herself, but he *had* danced with her and it was a memory she would treasure for the rest of her days.

Suddenly as she heard the sound of the door being opened very gently Drina snapped out of her reverie and sat up in the bed. Louisa. Of course. She would without doubt want a coze on this of all nights. As a crack of light appeared in the doorway Drina whispered, "Louisa?", but there was no reply, and then, recalling that they had adjoining rooms and that Louisa would have come through the connecting door, she felt a quiver of unease.

A shadow appeared in the doorway, one that

bore no resemblance to her cousin, and then, as the door closed again, there was only darkness.

"Who is it?" she asked, and her trembling voice betrayed her fear.

"Don't be afraid, I will not harm you."

A man! Perspiration broke out on her brow as she shrank further into the corner of the four-poster.

"Go away," she pleaded, and then with trembling hands she managed to light a candle. It was really not sufficient to light the room, but at least when she looked again she could now see who her visitor was and the darkness would no longer aggravate her terror. As the room grew lighter she looked round, and then her eyes became wide with shock.

"Lord Arundale!"

He took a step forward. "Please, Miss . . . it's Miss Alcott isn't it? Don't give the alarm, I beg you. I mean you no harm."

"Why are you here?"

She was terribly afraid. She knew of the morals of some bucks of the *ton*, but she had placed Lord Arundale above the behaviour she knew was indulged by those young men—especially those in her cousin Hugo's set—although she had no real reason to believe his morals were any better than theirs, and there was a distinct possibility that he might be drunk.

"I assure you, Miss Alcott, I didn't intend

to come in here. In fact, I thought this room was empty." He looked away. "I . . . became lost on my way to my room," he went on to explain with a degree of uncertainty Drina guessed was totally out of character. "It would be . . . embarrassing to be discovered abroad at this time of the night," he ended lamely. "I hope I did not alarm you too much."

"Only for the moment."

Drina noted the way he was dressed and understood only too well. Her cheeks flamed and she was glad of the poor lighting which would disguise it. She wondered which of the ladies in the party had been expecting his visit. She looked away in confusion. How foolish of her, she thought, to put him above such behaviour, commonplace as it was. Yet she did owe him something after his kindness tonight, for her happy memories, and even though it was totally improper for him to be in her room she would neither reveal his presence nor cause him embarrassment by insisting that he must leave before it was safe for him to do so.

"I will not give the alarm," she said at last, still avoiding looking him.

When he answered, "I am most obliged to you; it could have been dev'lish awkward," there was no mistaking the relief in his voice, and she was glad she was in a position to help him.

He listened at the door for a moment or two

and then said, "I will not stay longer than is necessary, Miss Alcott," and when she made no answer to this he said, "You are Lady Lythe's companion, are you not?"

At this she turned and glared at him, tossing back her head in defiance. "I am not! I happen to be Sir Arthur's niece. My mother was his sister."

He was taken aback more by her ferocity than his mistake. "I most humbly beg your pardon, ma'am. I thought . . ."

She relaxed then, her dark locks fanning out against the pillow. "There is some justification in what you thought, Lord Arundale. I am only a poor relation . . ."

He came across the room and stood looking down on her. "Why on earth does she treat you so badly?"

Forgetting her embarrassment, she looked at him imploringly. "I cannot conceive what you may mean, my lord. Aunt Constance is kindness itself to me. I am very for . . ."

At that moment the connecting door opened hesitantly and Drina's eyes opened wide in horror once more as she saw Louisa framed in the doorway, candle in hand.

"I thought I heard . . ."

The Earl whirled round on his heel and when Louisa saw the two of them she almost dropped the candle. "Drina! Lord Arundale!" she gasped, looking from one to the other in astonishment and horror. And then, as she stared at her cousin, her face began to crumple. "Oh, Drina, how *could* you?"

"Louisa, it isn't . . ."

But Louisa wasn't listening; she turned on her heel and ran back into her room. Drina turned her fear-filled eyes to the Earl, who appeared to have been turned to stone.

"Lord Arundale, you must stop her! Explain to her. Oh, hurry before she rouses the entire household!"

At such urgency in her voice he moved at last, but just as Drina was about to get out of her bed and follow also he returned. His face looked ashen in the candlelight and his proud stance was for once stooped.

"She has gone before I could stop her. I think she must have gone to rouse someone."

Drina covered her face with her hands. "Oh, Lord Arundale, what are we to do? There will be the most awful scandal. Your reputation . . ."

"My reputation, you must see, can hardly be marred. It is yours which is in jeopardy."

She was almost paralysed with fear. "Surely no one could believe you were here . . ."

He hesitated and then came across the room. He sat down on the bed next to her. "Please do not distress yourself, Miss Alcott. I will do all I can to avert any scandal and the loss of your own reputation."

"You must explain why you are here," she said breathlessly.

There was a moment's pause and then he answered in a very soft voice, "I cannot." She looked at him. "In any event, it will not make any difference. I am here in your room and for whatever reason we are compromised. It is my fault entirely, Miss Alcott, and I assure you I shall bear the consequences myself."

Before she could question him further there came a scream and she looked up, the Earl looked around and there stood Lady Lythe in the doorway. She was clad in her nightgown, a shawl clutched around her. Her iron-grey curls were neatly imprisoned under her cap which had somehow become askew, and behind her loomed the bulk of Sir Arthur whose face was brick red.

"Arundale! I'll have your hide for this, you scoundrel!"

The young man got quickly to his feet. "Sir Arthur," he began, but he was not allowed to continue.

Lady Lythe stormed into the room, glaring at her niece. "You brazen hussy! How dare you cause this scandal when your cousin is about to be married."

"Aunt Constance. . . ."

"There will be no scandal, Lady Lythe," the Earl said in an authoritative voice, "so please be so good as to stay silent and no one but the five of us will know of it."

"That is all very well, Arundale," Sir Arthur began, "but my niece's reputation . . ."

He began to move towards the door. "No one will care a fig about her reputation when she becomes my wife, sir." And bowing curtly, saying, "We will discuss the matter in the morning, Sir Arthur. Good night, ladies," he marched out of the room.

He left behind him a stunned silence, and then Sir Arthur, Lady Lythe and their daughter began to talk all at once, until Drina cried out in anguish, "It is all a terrible mistake!" and burst into tears.

Sir Arthur murmured, "Well, that makes all the difference, I must own." He laughed gruffly. "Was afraid for a moment I might have to challenge the fellow to a duel, and he's a dev'lish good shot."

"Oh, nonsense, Arthur," his wife answered peevishly. "I wouldn't allow you to duel over Drina."

Louisa now burst into tears too, crying, "It was all my fault," and turning on her heel she fled into her own room, sobbing heartbrokenly.

This, of course, diverted her mama, who followed her, crooning soothingly. "Don't cry, my pet. You are blameless. You will have red eyes in the morning and you wouldn't want Harborough to see you with red eyes, my love . . ."

Sir Arthur looked embarrassed for a moment left with his niece whom he had never before seen less than composed.

"I'll bid you good night, m'dear. Mustn't wake the entire household, eh? That wouldn't do at all."

When the only reply was more intense sobbing on his niece's part, he cleared his throat and went back into his daughter's room, closing the door behind him. Moments later Drina jumped out of the bed and locked both doors before throwing herself back on to the counterpane and sobbing even harder.

Drina was up very early the following morning, which was neither difficult nor surprising, for she had not slept at all. Despite this, the events of the night had taken on a dreamlike quality in her mind; that dreadful scene could not possibly have happened.

Except for the stirrings of the servants, the house was still silent when Drina came out of her room and she knew that few enough of the guests would venture abroad before midmorning. As she came down the stairs into the great marble hall an army of servants not normally seen above stairs were already hard at work, scrubbing and polishing.

This morning Drina was dressed in a gingham gown with a high ruff neck, and around her shoulders she had thrown a paisley shawl to ward off the chill of the morning, for there was nothing she wanted more than fresh air after her sleepless night. There had been rain during the night, she noted as she stood on the topmost of the steps which led down to the driveway, although she had been unaware of anything other than the storm in her own life at the time. There were pools of water everywhere, glistening in the sun.

As she stood there she saw a solitary rider in the distance and realised she was not alone in being up early. Lady Hélène Petley, whom Drina admired so much, was out riding, for the green habit against the red of her hair was unmistakable. But it was strange that she should ride alone without so much as a groom for company. However, Drina reasoned, she was a married lady and no doubt not riding far.

Married. The thought made her heart turn over and she quickly went down the steps. He could not really intend to go so far as to *marry* her. And yet he had said so, and for a man of honour there was no alternative. She wandered into the formal garden which at this time of the year was no longer at its best. The trees and flowers looked faded and forlorn, which did nothing to cheer or reassure her. The air was more chill and winter was on its way. There was the feeling of decay in the air. All at once it was too overpowering for her and she walked quickly back to the house, realising that the satin pumps she was wearing were quite inappropriate for the weather conditions and were already quite soaked through to her silk stockings.

Two carriages now stood in front of the house, one a racing curricle with a team of splendid horses champing at the bit, and the other a statelier carriage which was being loaded with baggage by Lord Southway's lackeys. Drina walked round them slowly, consumed with curiosity and more than a little dread, for both carriages bore the coat of arms of the Earl of Arundale.

As she stared at them the Earl himself came out of the house and paused on the top step. Her first panic-stricken impulse was to run and hide as she had as a child when Hugo and his friends tormented her, but common sense prevailed and with a greater degree of courage than anyone could have imagined she went forward to meet him.

He was dressed for travelling, she noted, wearing a caped driving coat and a curly-brimmed beaver which he doffed to her as she came towards him. His riding whip, silver-capped, and his gloves were clutched in his hand and she couldn't help but think how handsome he was, how well he wore his clothes. His coats sat well on those muscular shoulders and unlike Hugo's, his skin-tight pantaloons needed no padding.

"Good morning, Miss Alcott," he said, regarding her with a coldness which dashed all such thoughts from her head.

"Good morning, Lord Arundale," she replied, forcing herself to look into his face. It was a great effort. "You . . . you are leaving, I see."

He smiled grimly. "I have just finished conferring with Sir Arthur. The arrangements are made."

"Arrange . . . ments?" she stammered.

"I hardly think I need explain, Miss Alcott," he said, his manner even colder now. "I am going directly to London to open up my house there, and then on to Cheltenham to visit my grandmother." For a moment he looked away, his hands tightening on the whip. Drina had the oddest feeling he would like to have used it on someone, perhaps even on her. "I would rather," he went on a moment later, "her hear the news from me than from anyone else."

"Surely there is little chance of that in Cheltenham."

His eyes were very dark as they came to rest on her face once more. The effect was to make her shiver slightly, but that might have been because of the cool breeze which was blowing.

"My grandmother manages to keep abreast of all news, even in Cheltenham."

They were standing under the portico of the

main entrance to the house, both of them dwarfed by the large edifice. Drina bit her lip and he went on, "Sir Arthur knows of my movements and will set a date in accordance with them. I have instructed him to provide you with everything you require."

As he spoke, her carefully preserved calm began to crumble. "But I don't want to get married!" she cried, and then added in a softer voice, "At least, not in these circumstances."

"And I, Miss Alcott, do not wish to get married in any circumstances, but there is no alternative as you must already know."

He drew on his gloves as a footman approached. "All is in readiness, my lord," he said, and the Earl nodded.

Drina felt too choked with emotion to speak. He glanced down at her feet. "You would do well to change your pumps before you catch cold," he said and, placing his beaver on top of a mass of dark, pomaded curls, he strode down the steps to where his curricle waited.

She didn't look round or wait until he had gone before running into the house. More of the guests were coming down now and she was forced to move more decorously for fear of them suspecting something was amiss. She managed to bid them all, "Good morning," and smiled until her face felt as if it might crack. At last she reached her aunt's room and was relieved to find her up and having her hair dressed by her maid, Adams.

Lady Lythe displayed no pleasure at seeing her niece, and Drina as usual expected none. "Oh, so it is you," she said, turning her attention back to her mirror.

"Aunt Constance, I must talk with you," she answered, twisting her hands together in silent anguish.

"Yes," Lady Lythe agreed with a sigh, "there is a great deal to discuss, I must own, Drina, and we may as well do it now as later. Sit down. Sir Arthur is very satisfied, as well we might all be in the circumstances."

For once Drina did not obey her aunt, for she could not sit down. She walked across to the window with its view of the lake. It was a peaceful sight and did much to calm her agitation.

"You look awful, Drina. Did you know that?"

"I haven't slept at all."

"Perhaps that signifies that you have a conscience somewhere beneath all that arrogance you inherited from your mother." Drina was about to make a retort, but then Lady Lythe turned to look at her. "How long has this . . . relationship been going on, madam?"

Drina's eyes opened wide. "Relationship, Aunt?"

Lady Lythe made a noise of impatience.

"Don't look so innocent. You know perfectly well what I mean. Your . . . relationship with Lord Arundale. Not long, I trust."

Drina shook her head wildly. "There is no relationship, Aunt. It wasn't like that at all."

"Anyway, you are to be the Countess of Arundale, so I do not suppose it will matter, but whoever would have credited such a thing? I hope, madam, you will not forget your relatives and all they have done for you in your elevated position."

"Of course not, Aunt Constance." She turned to look out of the window again, her fingers absently twisting strands of the fringe on her shawl around and around. "Aunt Constance, all this talk of marriage to Lord Arundale is ridiculous and you know it. I don't want to marry him!"

Her aunt stared at her in astonishment. "What nonsense is this?" She glanced at her maid, who was listening to the exchange with wide-eyed interest. "You may go now, Adams. I shall not require you again this morning." The woman obeyed, albeit reluctantly, and then Lady Lythe turned her full wrath upon her niece. "And do you suppose you have any choice in the matter, you ungrateful wretch? Mr Kingsby is one thing—Sir Arthur was foolish enough to allow you to refuse so good a man— but Lord Arundale . . . ! You must have taken leave of your senses. Lord Arundale at least is gentleman enough to know what is the right thing to do, so you will marry him, and make no mistake about *that*."

She nodded her head vigorously to give weight to her words, and Drina said in a pitiful voice, "It was all a mistake, Aunt. It was not as it appeared."

"You were compromised and so you must marry. I don't think you fully realise the seriousness of what occurred last night. I grant you Lord Arundale is man enough to turn any silly chit's head and with enough address to cause you to do wrong, but the consequences could be dire. In a month or two who is to know what may not transpire?"

Lady Lythe turned away from her niece and began to brush rouge on to her cheeks as Drina's eyes opened wide in horror. "Aunt Constance!"

The woman was still indignant. "In any event," she went on before Drina could protest further, "such an opportunity will never come *your* way again, my girl."

"It was a *mistake*."

"Perhaps a mistake that you were discovered, but be thankful for it. I don't think you realise how lucky you are. Oh," she went on in desperation, throwing down the pot of rouge, "you were never thankful for anything. You are just like your mother. She thought of no one but herself as long as I knew her. She was never content with what she had; she had to have more, and just at the very moment she wanted it. She didn't care a jot about the family, left to face their friends when she ran off with your father. We were forced to stay buried in the country and never really took our place in Society until this last Season. You are just the same, not a thought for others. . . ."

Drina clasped her hands together in front of her and clamped her lips together to force back a retort. She had heard it all before.

"Think of us, Drina, if this scandal were to become public. What then, I ask you?"

"But it wouldn't . . ."

"How can one tell? Lord Arundale is behaving in a perfectly honourable way and it would become you better too if you were to be a little more humble. You have not uttered one word of contrition . . ."

"I am sorry, sorry for the whole affair, but I have done nothing wrong . . ."

Her aunt eyed her coldly. "You really are the most brazen hussy I have ever had the misfortune to meet. Do you think I didn't notice the way you flirted with him last night in the most shameless way?"

Drina drew back. "I have never flirted with anyone in my life."

"Do not contradict me, Drina! I will not have it even if you are to become the Countess of Arundale. Do you hear me?" She waved a hand in the air. "Call it what you will, it amounts to . . . encouragement. One cannot blame Lord Arundale for believing . . ."

Drina was momentarily speechless, and then the door burst open and Louisa came rushing in. "Papa has just told me the news! Everyone is talking about it in the breakfast-room, for it is the greatest surprise to them all, of course."

She flung herself into Drina's arms. "Oh, my love, it is marvellous news, isn't it?"

For once Drina was not able to respond to her cousin's impetuosity. "Marvellous! Oh, Louisa, how can you say so? It's a disaster, and it is all your fault. If only you hadn't jumped to conclusions last night this would never have happened."

The girl shrank away from her, her blue eyes filling with tears. "Please don't be angry with me, Drina. I hardly knew what to think or what to do when I saw you both together."

"Now, no one is blaming you, my pet," her mother crooned, casting a furious look at Drina. "You did what you had to do, and you were perfectly correct."

Drina, who could never bear to see her cousin unhappy, relented immediately. "Aunt Constance is right, Louisa, it was not your fault."

The girl smiled tremulously. "Last night I felt so *wretched* about the whole affair, but now it is all right because you're going to be married. He's so handsome, Drina, and rich too!

I couldn't have chosen anyone better for you myself. I'm so glad for you."

Lady Lythe came to look at her daughter critically. "You don't look too hag-ridden, my dear, which is most surprising after having your sensibilities shattered last night."

Louisa's eyes shone brightly. "I had to come, Mama; I was so excited, but now I must go. Harborough is taking me riding after breakfast."

Her mother watched her fondly as she hurried from the room. She looked delightful, a slight figure in a velvet riding habit. But Lady Lythe's expression hardened again after her daughter had gone.

"Louisa was shattered last night, you know. I really thought she might come down with a fever. For some reason she has always looked up to you, Drina." Lady Lythe continued to look disapprovingly at her niece. "And she really is so unselfish. Even now she cannot conceive that your wedding will completely eclipse her own."

Drina put two hands to her cheeks. "Oh, no, that cannot be so."

"The wedding of the Earl of Arundale, even though he has insisted it be a quiet affair, cannot go without notice."

Drina was angry again, so angry she was trembling. "You are talking cruel nonsense, Aunt. How can this travesty of a wedding compare with Louisa's, where everyone will be in favour of it and happy about it? At this wedding no one, not even the bride and 'groom, wants it."

And without waiting for her aunt's angry response, Drina ran out of the room, slamming the door behind her.

FOUR

THE Earl of Arundale drove his team relentlessly even though with every mile passed he felt less like facing his grandmother with his unwelcome news. His mood since setting out from London had veered between extremes of anger (at Fate) and despondency about the future.

One matter he had decided upon; although circumstances forced him to bestow his good name on this nondescript creature, this distasteful marriage would make no difference at all to his lifestyle. In his eyes she would remain Miss Drina Alcott and he would still regard himself as a bachelor and enjoy such freedom as this estate allows.

Before leaving London, the Earl had ensured that his Grosvenor Square house was in order to receive its new mistress in due course—he would naturally accord Miss Alcott every consideration necessary for appearances to the world. Because she was innocent of blame in this matter he could hardly do less. He had originally planned to hide her permanently at Arundale Park, but on realising such a course would give rise to precisely the kind of gossip and speculation he was anxious to avoid, he had decided to have as normal a marriage as possible. Somehow he believed Miss Alcott would be amenable to any course he suggested, which soothed his wounded sensibilities to some small degree.

Prior to setting out on his journey the Earl had also sent a note to Sir Francis Petley's house, assuring him that all was well with Lady Petley and that she was missing him. He also steeled himself to add a paragraph informing him of the forthcoming wedding and the Earl believed it was the very first time there had been a secret between the two, but he was determined that Francis should never learn the reason why the marriage had been contracted. The knowledge could only lead to Sir Francis feeling unnatural guilt over the affair.

The Dowager Countess of Arundale had lived in a modest manner in Cheltenham for some years past, firmly believing that the waters benefited her rheumatics which daily rendered her more inactive. A maidservant the Earl had never seen before seemed overawed at the sight of him, but she recovered sufficiently to show him into the drawing-room which was situated on the ground floor.

Miss Rowlands, the Countess's companion of many years, was reading a chapter from one of Miss Austen's novels to his grandmother when he was announced. The woman immediately jumped to her feet and the Earl smiled as the familiar acid tones of his grandmother's voice filled the room.

"What is it, Rowlands? Why have you stopped? Does it bore you too now? And about time too. Find me something more interesting."

"Your ladyship, the Earl is here."

The old lady squinted in his direction. "Simon? Is it really you?"

"Yes, Grandmama," he answered, coming further into the room.

"How good it is to see you, and so unexpectedly. Such treats do my heart good."

He came to take her hands and kissed the dry, wrinkled cheeks. She looked more frail than ever now, huddled into the corner of a chair, warmly wrapped in a blanket.

"My eyes are not so good these days," she complained. "I am growing old."

"You look very well."

He glanced at Miss Rowlands, who said,

"The Countess has been troubled with the rheumatics, Lord Arundale, but otherwise she has been very well since you were last here."

The Countess gave a dry laugh. "The waters are not so good as they used to be." She waved a gnarled hand at her companion. "Be off with you, woman. Can't you see I want a coze with m'grandson?"

The woman scuttled away, and the Earl said softly, "I see you are still bullying her, Grandmama."

"Bah! She bullies *me*! Reads me Austen when I tell her not to. She thinks it is good for me. I ask you, Simon, Austen!"

"And you much prefer Mrs Radclyffe."

"Yes, by jove!" she answered, banging her stick on the floor. "Or Scott. Blood and thunder, m'boy." There was a momentary silence. "It's good to see you, Simon. Come and sit by me so I can see you better." He did so. "Now, what has brought you away from the Prince and that rackety crowd of his? Bah! He's not like his father. Georgie's a gentleman, as I often told him, and a good family man. Excellent example to the country. Poor devil. His attic's to let now."

She shook her head. "I have some news for you, Grandmama," he said, watching her indulgently.

"News? Don't tell me Boney's on the loose again. War again, is it? Speak up, boy."

He laughed. "No, Grandmama, Boney is still safe on Elba, where he will remain."

"Don't you believe it."

"I'm to be married."

There was a momentary silence during which he thought the old lady drew a sharp breath. "After all this time I never thought you would."

"Neither did I."

There was a momentary pause before she said, "Well, Simon, I am still waiting to be assured that you are not going to indulge that bitterness of yours by bringing some lightskirt into the forefront of Society."

Sombrely he answered, "I would not do anything to dishonour the family name. You need have no fear; she is perfectly respectable. Her name is Drina Alcott."

"Alcott? Alcott? Don't know any Alcotts. Who the devil is she?"

"She comes from a good family. The Lythes."

"Ah, yes, I knew a Sir Frederick Lythe once. Dull fellow. Must be her grandfather. Reminded me of a Methodist minister. Never did like him. When's it to be?"

"Soon. I have left the arrangements to her uncle, Sir Arthur Lythe, who is her guardian."

"Well, it isn't before time. I'd long since given up hope of seeing m'great-grandchildren, I don't mind admitting. It has been a grief to me. Didn't want the line to die out, Simon.

"What portion does she have? Estates too, of course."

"No, Grandmama."

"None at all?" Her voice was like the croaking of a frog. "I find that hard to credit."

"She comes from the poor part of the family."

The Dowager Countess gave a most unlady-like snort. "Then I'll warrant she is uncommonly beautiful."

The Earl got up and walked across to the piano on which stood miniatures of members of his family, including one of his late mother who had been a beauty in her day. There was no point in hiding anything from this astute old lady, as had been painfully proved on many occasions in the past.

Keeping his back to her, he answered, "I believe you would find her presentable."

"*Presentable!*" she croaked, and then she began to cough. Immediately the Earl went to the sideboard and poured a glass of lemonade for her, but when he offered it to her she waved it away. "Porter. Bring me some porter. In the jug next to the lemonade."

"It is not good for you, Grandmama. Drink this instead."

Her face grew red. "Don't tell me what is good for me, boy. Bring me porter or I shall put my stick about your back!"

She went into a paroxym of coughing again, and the Earl deemed it prudent to obey. Several minutes later the Countess sank back into her chair, calm again but breathless.

"Shall I ring for Rowlands?" he asked hesitantly.

"Don't you dare! I don't want that Friday-faced creature around me more than is absolutely necessary. She bullies me and she's only waiting for me to die, you know."

"She is devoted to you."

"Shan't leave her anything in m'will. Get my own back that way. Hah!" She turned her myopic stare on her grandson again. "Well, hadn't you better tell me all about it?"

Sighing with resignation, he did so, omitting references to Sir Francis and Lady Petley, of course. As always in the presence of this awesome and dominating woman, he felt like a foolish little boy.

"A pretty little mess and no mistake," she said severely when he had finished.

"I had no choice but to ask for her hand."

She deliberated a moment before saying, "You did the proper thing, Simon. It's a mess, I don't deny," she gave a short, sharp and surprising burst of laughter, adding, "and now you will just have to make the best of it."

The Earl had been staring rigidly out of the carriage window ever since they had set off. Now London was well behind them and Arundale Park lay ahead. The thought filled Drina with dread. How on earth could she cope with being the Countess of Arundale? Even now it did not seem real.

She watched him fearfully, wondering what was going on in his mind, and if he were as dazed as she. It had all happened at such speed. The number and importance of the guests who had appeared at her wedding had surprised her, even being aware of the Earl's standing in Society. Even the Regent had put in a brief appearance and she had been terrified of him until his charm had put her at ease. All the same, it was an intimation of the grandeur of the Earl's mode of living which she would now have to share, and she was not at all sure she could grow accustomed to it.

"Everything went off very well," she ventured.

He turned at last to look at her and she suspected that he did not find what he saw much to his liking, even though her new fur-lined pelisse was a becoming shade of green which suited her well. Aunt Constance had been more inclined to indulge her niece's whims in the days before she became Lady Arundale, and Drina suspected the Earl's hand in the matter.

"I beg your pardon," he murmured. "I was thinking of . . ."

She had a vague idea what he might be thinking of; that beauty of long ago who should have been his bride. Drina thought about her constantly, wondering what could have induced her to prefer another man to one she was sure could have no equal.

Her thoughts, together with the attention he was now bestowing upon her, caused her cheeks to flush and she averted her eyes. "It was of no importance, Lord Arundale. I simply remarked that the wedding went off well."

He smiled grimly. "It did indeed."

There was a silence again during which he continued to study her, and this time it was Drina who took refuge in the scenery outside. Autumn was definitely here now; all the trees on the wayside were shedding their brown and gold leaves, bowing low before the wind that lashed them mercilessly. Inside Lord Arundale's luxurious carriage all was warm, except for Drina's heart. Two weeks ago, if anyone was to have asked her to make one wish it would have been to become the Countess of Arundale. Now she was willing to do anything to relieve him of his unwanted burden.

"Your cousin, I believe, was a trifle bosky," he ventured a moment later.

Drina gave him her attention once more and could not help but smile; he was as at a loss for words as she.

"Hugo could never hold his liquor."

"He must learn to control himself, but no

doubt time will take care of that." He looked at her with interest for the first time. "So your name is really Alexandrina."

"No one has called me anything other than Drina."

"Then I shall continue to do so. Nevertheless it was strange not to know of it until the wedding ceremony. It is an unusual name."

She smiled faintly. "My mother, I am told, was an unusual woman." She hesitated before saying, "I am also told that Arundale Park is a very fine mansion."

He seemed to relax. "You will get to know it well during our stay."

"Is it as large as Southways?"

"Oh, it is much larger. I go there often, as you will discover, mainly to attend to the stud farm and to ascertain the condition of my race-horses. We are quite close to Newmarket."

Drina listened avidly, anxious to learn all she could about him. When it became evident that she could not extricate herself from this imbroglio she vowed to do all in her power to serve him. She must, in the time to come, find the proper way to do so.

"There are a great many matters demanding my attention now," he went on, "so whilst I am going about my business you may learn to run the house. I have frequent house parties when the racing is on, and now I am married it might be possible to extend more invitations. It will not be a small task, though. Do you feel equal to it?"

He was watching her keenly as she nodded. "I did some housekeeping for my aunt. Of course, it was not on such a grand scale."

"I feel sure it will not be beyond you."

"I'm flattered." She glanced at him briefly before saying, "If you are to be concerned with your estate and I with the household management it will be an odd way to spend our honeymoon."

She averted her eyes as he drew in a sharp breath. "Let us be clear, Miss . . . Drina, there will be no honeymoon for us in the accepted sense. To the world we shall appear united, but otherwise we shall go our separate ways. No doubt that will be a relief to you also."

She nodded. "I appreciate that it will take time to grow to know each other."

"I fancy we shall have a lifetime in which to do that," he observed dryly, and Drina did not miss the irony in his voice. "When we return to London you have my permission to entertain as you see fit. Clothe yourself as befits my wife and have all the bills sent to me."

"Oh, that is very kind of you, but my uncle has already provided me with an assortment of clothes to serve as my trousseau. I believe in the circumstances that it will be sufficient."

He smiled again, a mite less grimly this time. "I see I shall have to find someone who will take you in hand. As my wife you . . ."

"But I shall not be your wife."

"To all intents and purposes you will be," he went on irritably. "Really, Drina, you will have to learn not to interrupt when I speak to you."

She averted her eyes again. "I beg your pardon, Lord Arundale. Please continue."

"Thank you. I should hate to have married a prattle box."

Her cheeks grew pink. "I assure you, Lord Arundale, I am used to speaking only when addressed."

He then looked contrite. "I did not mean to be unkind, but as I was saying, as my wife you will require rather special clothes for all occasions. You may also engage or hire any extra servants you feel you need either in London or in Suffolk. It is not a favour, I assure you, but a right to which you are entitled."

Drina began to play with her muff. "Is this person you would have take me in hand your grandmother?"

"Good Lord, no!" he cried as the carriage passed over a rough part of the road and shook them about. Drina clung on to the strap. "My grandmother is very old and lives in Cheltenham. We shall probably visit her in the spring."

"Is that why she was not present today and not because she was . . . displeased about our marriage?"

The Earl looked vexed at being quizzed by her. "The reason she did not attend is because she is far too frail to travel these days."

"You have so few relatives, my lord."

"You must learn to call me Simon." She blushed, and he went on quickly, "I am the only child of an only child. My grandmother had several children, but only my father survived to become an adult and marry. My own mother died before I could even remember her, and my father did not marry again."

"Do you not wish to . . . perpetuate your line?" she asked in a voice that was slightly breathless.

He gazed out of the window and she noticed that he looked vexed again. Drina was afraid her very existence must annoy him now, but she could not find it in her heart to blame him. He must have had so many wonderful hopes and plans once when he was young and in love with a sought-after beauty.

"Why should I care what happens to my possessions once I am dead?"

"I . . . don't know, but most men do care."

"It is the present which concerns me most of all. I have never understood those men who have married simply to provide themselves with heirs who promptly gamble away their inheritance and ruin the property left to them."

There was a silence between them for a moment or two, and then Drina said, "I am an only child too, but luckily for me Mama had a brother who cared for us when Papa died."

He looked at her with interest once more. "Tell me why you had such an invidious position in his household."

"Invidious, Lord . . . Simon?" She thought he frowned at the familiar use of his name, but he *had* insisted, she reasoned. "Uncle Arthur has always treated me as a daughter."

"If that is the case, it is certainly not true of your aunt. No, do not deny it, Drina, for I know it is true. Your loyalty does you credit, so you may speak of it this once and I shall never allude to it again."

Drina sighed. "She always believed she was being kind to me. She never looked for the responsibility of someone else's child."

Suddenly she began to laugh, and he frowned. "Pray allow me to enjoy the joke too."

"I was just wondering who Aunt Constance will send for her Hungary water or her vinaigrette now I am gone." Immediately she looked contrite. "Such a thought is not worthy of me."

He smiled suddenly and he looked quite different. Gone was the severe expression she had grown used to; he looked young and carefree and she could almost imagine he liked her.

"No doubt she will find some poor creature, rather like the one my grandmother employs. Grandmama enjoys bullying the woman, and I rather believe Miss Rowlands enjoys being bullied."

He leaned forward in his seat. "How did it come about? I must know more about you, Drina. It is ludicrous that I do not."

"It is not an unusual story, I fear. My mother was the favourite in her family and when Lady Lythe married Sir Arthur she did not like it, naturally, being the wife of the elder son. Mama was very beautiful and she had many suitors, but when she did choose, it was . . . my father. There was nothing wrong with him; simply he had neither title nor fortune, just a great deal of love for her. Grandfather, it seems, would not hear of a match, so they ran away together." He was watching her woodenly, all sign of that brief friendliness gone completely. "Grandfather cut her out of his will, disowned her completely. When Papa died I was only two years old and there was no money left, so Mama had to throw herself upon Uncle Arthur's generosity. We went to live with him, but Mama died only two years later."

The Earl continued to stare at her, and then he picked up the book which lay on the seat at his side. "I think I shall read for the remainder of the journey before we stop for dinner."

And so saying, he opened the book, leaving Drina to stare out of the window at the grey, flat countryside.

FIVE

SOME three months later the Earl of Arundale considered he had cause to reflect that his marriage had not turned out as badly as he might have expected. True, it was not a marriage in every sense of the word, but the Earl guessed that his wife was glad about that too, and she had since proved to be the most sought-after hostess of the Season. Incredibly, invitations to their balls and assemblies were eagerly sought after even by the most jaded socialites. He was not sure how this state of affairs had come about—he had really feared that Drina would remain a dowd despite the money at her disposal—but all in all the Earl concluded it was a most satisfactory situation.

His house in Grosvenor Square on this occasion was packed with people, a glittering array of the richest and most influential in the land. The woman who stood at his side to receive their visitors was quite unlike the girl he had taken to Arundale Park immediately after their wedding, and now it was difficult to imagine her that mousy creature content to remain in the background whilst her cousin attracted all the attention.

On their return to London it had been Lady Petley who had befriended the new Countess and it had been she with her innate French flair who had guided Drina's trips to the Bond Street shops and Pall Mall emporiums, and as a result the Countess of Arundale was one of the best-dressed hostesses in London.

Tonight she sparkled almost as brightly as her diamond tiara or the emeralds which were clasped about her throat and wrists. The Earl watched her in conversation with the Duke of Fordingham, who was dressed in the extreme style of the dandies. He had abominable taste in clothes, but he was obviously bewitched by Drina.

"Made a wise choice there," Sir Francis observed as he came up to his friend. "Prinny's absolutely entranced."

The Earl chuckled. "So I observed the other evening at Carlton House, but don't you think those gatherings grow a little too extravagant now?"

"Perhaps," the other mused, "but I doubt if even Parliament could prevail upon him to be more circumspect now. Hélène's very fond of the Countess too, you know."

The Earl drew his gaze away from his wife at last. "They get on famously. I'm glad, Francis. I believe they were both in need of a friend."

"Strange how we never noticed her much before," Sir Francis mused as they looked at Drina once more. "She's quite a beauty. You were clever to notice it." He turned to the Earl again. "Just think, Simon, you might never have offered for her if it hadn't been for me."

His friend was startled as Sir Francis slapped him on the shoulder. "You, Francis? What *do* you mean?"

Sir Francis laughed, but it was lost in the general mêlée of noise in the drawing-room. "Southways. You were going to cry off. Remember? You only went to keep an eye on Hélène for me."

The Earl drew a sigh. "I remember." He looked at his friend. "How is Hélène now?"

The other man smiled weakly. "Oh, I doubt if I shall ever know her well, Simon. She has such dark moods, I cannot possibly understand them. She's French, of course, and perhaps that is the answer; they are a volatile race. I shall always be jealous, though."

"Coming to Newmarket next week?"

Sir Francis brightened. "Wouldn't miss it. What you racing?"

"Malmina. She's in great form just at the moment."

"It will do Hélène the world of good to go to the country. Delicate nerves, you know. Not surprising after the hellish time she had in Paris. . . . If only I were sure it was only that."

"If there were more, Francis, Drina would know it, and if it were not to Lady Petley's credit my wife would not remain silent."

"Women talk, don't they?"

The Earl smiled. "A great deal."

"Perhaps the Countess is in her confidence and would know."

The Earl fixed him with a steely eye. "No, Francis."

"Just lead the conversation round to it, that's all I ask."

Recalling the last time he agreed to help his friend, the Earl simply laughed and tapped him on the arm. "I have promised the Duchess of Portchester my arm into supper. Wouldn't do to be late."

The Countess of Arundale glanced around the crowded supper-room and drew a sigh of satisfaction that yet another of her assemblies was a success. Becoming so successful a hostess had not been easy for her after the life she had previously led and she had been hampered at first by a certain amount of natural shyness, but she had worked hard to become what she believed her husband wanted of her. On the day of her marriage Drina had vowed never to be anything but a credit to him and as she exchanged a brief smile with him across the room she knew she had succeeded. He was pleased with her and perhaps a little surprised.

As he returned to his conversation with a group of his racing friends she took the opportunity of studying him. Her heart beat unevenly each time she was near to him and tonight even more so, for he looked so handsome in his dark evening coat. No other man could compare, and although there were at least six men present anxious to become her lover, Drina would have nothing to do with them. There had been only one man in her life, which was ironic. To the world they were an ideal couple, envied by many, and Drina supposed she must be satisfied with that.

It seemed incredible that only a few short months ago she had craved in the most secret place in her heart for this kind of position in Society, and now, having achieved it, she would gladly give everything away, position, title, jewels and clothes, just to have his love. Admiration and kindness, Drina was coming to recognise, just were not enough. At all times he was pleasant to her and considerate in the extreme, but always he was stiff and withdrawn. He never addressed her in a manner warmer than that he would adopt to a stranger; that at least had not changed. She longed to see him unbend towards her, to look at her with some small degree of warmth in those dark eyes. . . .

"With a splendid rout," Louisa said breathlessly as she came up to her, startling her cousin out of her unwelcome thoughts.

Drina recovered herself immediately and smiled fondly at the girl. "I'm glad you are enjoying it."

"And you look so splendid," she added in a whisper. "Mama is quite *green* with envy over your jewels."

"They belong to the Arundale family, not to me."

"It is the same thing. Your gown is magnificent, Drina! Mama says you must tell me your dressmaker so I too can engage her."

"I will send her to you."

"You're so good, Drina, and I'm so glad you won't have to go back to Rington Manor after I am married."

Drina laughed. "So am I. And it will not be

long before you too set up your own establishment."

"Six weeks! Oh, here comes Mama now." She clutched at her cousin's arm and said in a whisper, "Drina, may I call on you tomorrow? Alone. Early."

Drina gazed at her questioningly. "You need never ask, Louisa. I am always at home to you."

"Harborough is looking for you," Lady Lythe told her daughter in a severe tone, and after she had scampered away the matron looked at her niece. "You are looking very well, Drina."

"Thank you, Aunt Constance."

"I should also like to say that I think you have contrived very well too in your new life."

Drina didn't know whether her tone implied surprise or disappointment; she suspected a little of both.

"I was just remarking to Louisa that she will soon be opening her own establishment."

Lady Lythe fanned herself furiously and the feathers in her turban nodded in unison. "It will not be until next Season. They intend to travel on the Continent for several months after the wedding. But you know," she went on, looking at her niece, "I doubt if she will be able to become a brilliant hostess; Louisa hasn't your . . . dedication."

"I will do all I can to help her, Aunt."

"I am obliged."

Drina watched her stomp away and shook her head in amazement at how strange life could be. To think that Aunt Constance might have cause to be grateful to her. But Drina was glad to be of service to her family, for it was little enough to repay for her upbringing in their home.

The supper-room was emptying now and she concentrated on circulating amongst her guests, many of whom were attached to the military or the diplomatic corps and had recently returned from the Congress of Vienna. It provided a good talking point. Although ostensibly a meeting of the Allies to decide the future of Europe, it seemed no more than an excuse for revelry.

Before long all the guests had gone into the drawing-room to resume the singing, dancing or card-playing now in progress, and Drina remained to give brief instructions to the footmen. It was when she was about to go back to join her guests that she met her cousin, Hugo, as he walked unsteadily towards the supper-room.

"Where's the champagne?" he demanded in a slurred voice.

"I think you have had enough," she answered, and would have gone past him had he not caught her arm.

"The Countess of Arundale," he said, "is renowned for her open-handed hospitality."

"I am gratified indeed. It still remains, Hugo, that you are drunk."

He laughed. "Think I can't take it, don't you?"

"I know you can't. Hugo, come along with me to the drawing-room and I shall get you some lemonade."

He laughed again. "You really are impressive, Dory. Who'd think it? That skinny little girl who always ran away from me when I caught her alone in the library."

"If your father had known about it he would have whipped you."

He grinned and almost toppled over. "Then why did you never tell him? You've turned into a great woman, Dory, but you know that, don't you?"

"Hugo, let me go."

But he showed no disposition to do so. He ran one hand along her bare shoulder. "It is quite wonderful what some good clothes and a few thousand guineas' worth of jewels can do for any woman."

"You're insulting, Hugo. Now, let go."

His leering face, the smell of alcohol seemed very near. "Now how could I possibly insult you, Dory? My dear cousin who was found with a man in her bedroom."

Drina's face flooded with colour. "You forget yourself!"

"No, it is you who does that, my fine beauty," he said softly, running his hand on her bare flesh once more, causing her to flinch away from him, "but I do know who you are. You're my little cousin, so forget all your recently acquired airs and give me a kiss."

He pushed his face into hers and pinned her, still protesting, against the wall. Suddenly a hand clamped down on his shoulder and pulled him away from her quite viciously. Drina whirled round to see her husband, his face suffused with colour, clutching on to Hugo.

"You will apologise to my wife, Lythe, for your insulting behaviour," he said in a furious voice.

"She's my cousin. Only wanted a kiss."

The Earl shook him vigorously. "This is the Countess of Arundale you are addressing and don't you ever forget it, Lythe. An apology, you puppy, or I shall give you a whipping you will never forget."

Drina straightened her gown and her tiara, and composed herself once more. "It is of no moment, Simon. Let him go."

The Earl did so, and the frightened young man smoothed the wrinkles from his coat. Keeping his eyes downcast, he mumbled, "Beg pardon, my lady."

The Earl relaxed as he called for his butler. "In future you would do well to remember your manners.

"Ah, Lawrence, see that Captain Lythe is escorted home safely. He is feeling unwell."

Hugo allowed himself the indignity of being

escorted by the butler, and after he had gone Drina said breathlessly, "There was no need to be so hard on him, Simon."

He was staring hard at Hugo's back and as Drina spoke he glanced at her. "If you defend him so fiercely, my dear, I shall begin to think you were enjoying his attentions."

Before the astonished Countess could reply her husband had taken her arm and was leading her back towards their guests. "I want to talk to you, Drina. We shall be going to Arundale Park next week for the racing."

Immediately she was diverted and her face was transformed into a smile of pleasure. "I am so glad, Simon."

His face relaxed too. "These past three months have been hard on you, haven't they?"

"You must know that I've enjoyed every moment of it."

"Well, there will be little enough respite for you at Arundale Park. There will be a large party."

"I shall enjoy the change. Do you wish to leave the guest list to me?"

He smiled. "I believe I can do so quite safely, my dear, but omit Captain Lythe. I don't like his manners."

"As you wish," she answered, her eyes downcast.

He glanced across the room to where Mr. Augustus Fine was in conversation with Lady

Petley, and after hesitating a moment he said, "You'd best extend an invitation to Mr Fine too."

"Yes, if you wish it."

"He expressed an interest in seeing my racing stables." He raised his quizzing glass and observed them in conversation for a moment or two. "Lady Petley seems rather subdued this evening, I notice."

Drina looked at him in surprise as he let the glass drop. "Yes, I have noticed that too, but she is normally of uncertain humours."

"Do you not know why?"

"She does not confide in me," she answered, glancing at him curiously.

"But you are both such close friends."

"I am very fond of her, and yet . . . she is a very private person. I really don't feel as if anyone could know her well."

The Earl peered at her again through his quizzing glass and then a moment later said, "I have not yet spoken to her this evening, so I think I had best correct that omission."

Mr Fine was obliging enough to give up his seat to the Earl and expressed delight at the forthcoming houseparty at Arundale Park when it was mentioned to him, and then he wandered away, leaving him in Lady Petley's company.

She smiled at him weakly as he said, "You are looking most charming tonight, Lady Petley."

"And you are very gracious, Lord Arundale. I am enjoying myself greatly."

The Earl realised that Lady Petley was not her usual ebullient self and he was suddenly glad that his own wife did not suffer such delicate sensibilities. However delightful the woman, he knew he should soon become out of patience with consistent ill-humours.

"Francis tells me that Vienna delighted you."

"Ah, yes," she sighed, "it was a great pleasure to be in so pleasant a city. Of course, Francis was so often occupied with his business. So many secrets to discuss, Lord Arundale." He laughed. "I do resent the life he leads away from me."

"It is understandable."

"I am not, you see, so independent as your own dear wife. I need my husband near to me at all times."

"His career is very demanding," the Earl replied soothingly, "but it is important to him nevertheless."

She appeared to be troubled again and a bleak look came into her eyes. "Yes, I know it." Suddenly she brightened and looked at him with interest then. "Lord Arundale, I believe that marriage has mellowed you."

He was visibly taken aback. "Is it very evident?"

She laughed, but it had a forced sound to it.

"Well, I think now you like me a little better than you once did."

He hardly knew how to reply, and she laughed again. "Now I have embarrassed you and I did not mean to, I assure you. It is understandable. You know so little about me and consider me not good enough for Francis." The Earl was deeply discomforted and about to protest when she raised her hand. "It is true, Lord Arundale. I am only too well aware of how unworthy I am of your dear friend."

Lord Arundale was, in fact, deeply moved by her honesty and as he got to his feet he raised her hand to his lips. "You are very worthy of him, Lady Petley, and no one is more aware of it than Francis."

There were tears in her eyes and her voice was choked as she said, "Thank you, Lord Arundale."

From across the room Drina heard Lady Petley's laughter and she looked to see that it was her husband who had caused it. Moments later she saw him kiss her hand and it seemed that her own heart was in her throat, threatening to choke her. She could not draw her eyes away from them. It was as if there was no one else in the room save for the beautiful French-woman and her husband. Hélène looked ethereal in buttercup-yellow sarsnet with a topaz collar against the white of her throat, and the Earl, gazing down at her, looked roguishly handsome as always.

Drina's mind went back to that night at Southways. She had never questioned where Simon had been going that night, but now she realised it could have been only Lady Petley's room, facing her own. The realisation was so shattering, the room began to swim around her. Hélène and Simon. Lovers.

"Lady Arundale, are you feeling faint?" asked one of her guests.

She managed to reassure all of those staring at her worriedly that she was indeed perfectly well, and then she excused herself. She needed air and she made her way towards the terrace, managing to ward off several people who wished to converse with her. She pulled the curtains apart blindly to escape her new knowledge and the smiles and facile chatter of her guests. No one was out there on a February evening, but it was solitude she needed then. It was bitterly cold on such an evening, but Drina did not notice it, even though the wind blew chill and she was clad only in a figure-hugging chiffon gown.

Simon and Hélène. Why hadn't she seen it before? she asked herself. But it would explain his concern for Lady Petley's state of mind this evening and his determination to oust Mr Fine from her side. Jealousy welled up inside her like a fire fanned by the wind, and yet she knew it was ludicrous to experience such an emotion. She had so much more than even one of her wildest dreams. All she lacked was his love and he had never given her any hope of that. Of course, Drina knew there must be women in his life—the Earl of Arundale was not known to be a monk—but she had envisaged women in unspeakable establishments far removed from the fashionable world of Mayfair, women who would mean nothing to him. And Drina told herself it wouldn't matter, if she didn't know. . . .

Hélène was different; Hélène who had been so good a friend. Drina brushed away a tear, knowing she was being both foolish and ungrateful to feel such passion. It betrayed, she acknowledged, a lack of maturity and sophistication. To most ladies of her acquaintance such a liaison would mean little as long as it was conducted discreetly; they would find compensation elsewhere. But this was not for her.

Her heart ached unbearably for the love she had never known, and for the friend she trusted. Now she would never feel the same towards either of them, ever again.

When Sir Francis Petley entered the drawing-room of his house in Manchester Square the very next afternoon, he found his wife stooping by the fire. As the door opened she sprang to her feet, forcing a smile to her face.

"Francis! How nice it is to see you home so early in the day."

"What were you doing so close to the fire?"

Her hands fluttered helplessly as she glanced at the leaping flames. "It was growing cold in here. I think it might snow yet."

He frowned, striding over to the fireplace where a few charred pieces of paper lay in the hearth. "You should have called for one of the servants."

She turned away from him. "It was such a small task."

"You might have soiled your dress, Hélène, or even burned your hands."

She twisted her hands together in anguish. "I will remember in future, Francis. It is such a fuss over so small a matter." She turned to look at him again, the strained smile on her face once more. "It is good that you are home."

She held out her hands to him and they went to sit on a sofa together. He brushed a stray hair away from her cheek. "It will be good to spend a few days at Arundale Park next week." She froze and then turned her face away from him. He frowned. "Hélène? Is something amiss?"

"I do not want to go to Arundale Park," she said in a broken voice.

He laughed in bewilderment. "Why on earth not?"

"Do I have to make an excuse to you, Francis?" she asked in a harsh voice. "I simply do not wish to go."

"But, Hélène . . . the Arundales are our closest friends. I have never missed a Kelvington Plate, or any of the important meetings for that matter, and I don't intend to begin now."

Her head was bowed and he put his hand on her shoulder. "Hélène, my love, what is it that's troubling you? Can you not tell me?"

"Nothing, nothing is troubling me. I simply do not wish to go."

He jumped to his feet. "Well, if you can give me no reason. . . . Hell's teeth, Hélène! I'm growing heartily tired of these ill-humours which afflict you with more and more frequency of late. Let me tell you I have no intention of crying off, not for so paltry a reason."

He strode across the room, his face dark with anger. His wife had rarely seen him so out of humour. Just as he reached the door she sprang to her feet and ran after him.

"Francis, don't go!" She clung on to his arm, pressing her face against his sleeve. "Don't be angry with me, I beg of you. I will do anything you want of me, only forgive me."

"Nothing to forgive," he answered gruffly. "I thought you and Drina Arundale were great friends."

"We are. You must disregard my ill-humours, Francis. I would never wish to distress you."

He bent to kiss her brow and after he had gone her reassuring smile faded. She looked troubled once more and as she walked slowly across the room she picked up the charred papers and threw them back into the blazing fire.

As a direct result of standing on the terrace on a freezing February evening Drina contracted a severe chill. It rendered her so ill that the Earl called in several eminent doctors, and when the Prince Regent heard of her illness he insisted on sending his own personal physician along to Grosvenor Square too. The medical men prescribed poultices and purges, and at last, after three days of high fever, Drina found herself on the way to recovery once more.

It was only after the worst was over that she discovered the number of callers who had come to Grosvenor Square bearing flowers and messages of goodwill during that time, and she was moved to hear of it. Heartening too was the fact that the Earl had also been most concerned, hardly leaving the house at all during the crisis, but now that was over he had resumed his interests. Previously Drina had never wondered where he might be, but now, as she lay in her bed receiving a seemingly never-ending stream of well-wishers, she did wonder where he had gone and with whom he might be.

One of those earliest to call was Lady Petley herself, full of sympathy and concern for her friend. It was difficult for Drina to speak to her with any pretence of normality and it was fortunate that the state of her health could answer for a great deal.

"*Ma pauvre cherie*," she crooned the moment she was shown into the bedroom. She placed a large bunch of daffodils at the end of the bed. "Are you feeling better now?"

"Much better."

"How silly you were to stand in the cold for so long. What were you thinking of?"

"It was warm in the room and I needed the air."

Lady Petley clucked her tongue. "Such foolhardiness." Then she smiled as she seated herself by the bed. "But I am glad to see you are much better. The poor Earl was so distraught."

"Was he?" she asked, without much interest. She wished only for Lady Petley to go and leave her to her brooding thoughts once more.

The Frenchwoman fidgeted with her gloves for a moment or two before asking, "Obviously, we shall not be going to Arundale Park next week after all."

"Oh, I hope to be recovered long before then, Hélène. The worst is over, and in a day or two I hope to resume normal activities." Lady Petley appeared to be taken aback by this announcement and Drina was forced to ask, "Do I look so ill?"

Lady Petley laughed and some of the strain went from her face. "One would hardly know you had been so ill. You are very pale, of course, but if you are so set on going, a few days at Arundale Park will soon put the bloom back into your cheeks. It must be a very important meeting at Newmarket. Lord Arundale does not race his animals every time there is a meeting."

"I don't know, Hélène. I really don't know much about my husband's activities at all. Since our marriage I do know he has only raced at the most important meetings."

There was a moment's hesitation before Lady Petley said, "Drina, you do not seem to mind Arundale's activities when he is not with you."

Drina looked at her sharply, but her eyes were downcast. "I really don't understand . . ."

"It is of no matter," she answered, smiling again. "I have no right to inflict my own megrims on you."

"If there is something troubling you, Hélène, perhaps you should tell me about it."

There was alarm in her eyes which brought an added heaviness to Drina's heart. She turned her face away from the other. "I am tired, Hélène. I would deem it a favour if you would leave me to rest now."

The woman hesitated and as the chair scraped

back on the floor she murmured, "I shall see you another time, *ma chère*. I fear I have tired you."

She was dressed in green silk with a matching pelisse edged with gold braid and a bonnet which framed her face and made her eyes seem larger and more lustrous. As she went from the room Drina turned her face into her pillow and a few tears escaped from the corners of her eyes.

The Earl, coming up the stairs, was surprised to see Lady Petley come out of his wife's room and brush away a tear from her cheek.

"Lady Petley," he greeted her cautiously, "I trust you do not find my wife worse?"

The woman was momentarily startled, and then she recovered herself. "No, indeed, she appears much improved. Weak, of course, but the truth is, Lord Arundale, I do not think I am too much in favour today." She started to move past him. "I am to meet Francis in a short time, so you must excuse me. Good day to you, Lord Arundale."

She hurried away, leaving the Earl to stare after her curiously before he continued on his way to his wife's room. He also found he was not in favour and he did not remain long at her side. Fortunately, the Duchess of Portchester and her daughter called, which gave the Earl a much-wanted opportunity to make his escape.

His experience was a little shattering, for he had rarely seen his wife so out of sorts.

Another constant visitor to Grosvenor Square during those days was Louisa who had, as promised, arrived at the Arundales' house the day after the rout to discover her cousin ill. She had endured an anxious few days, so that when she called in on one cold, sunny morning and found Drina reclining on a sofa in the drawing-room, she was delighted.

"Louisa, dearest, how kind of you to call. I was hoping to see you before long. Arundale tells me you were hardly absent from the house during the crisis."

"That is true, but my engagement book has been so full these past few days I haven't had a chance to call round since, which has been most vexing to me."

Louisa's arms were filled with books she had chosen from the circulating library and the latest edition of the *Ladies' Magazine*. Once she had divested herself of these gifts she came to kiss Drina on the brow, saying, "I was quite loth to leave you at all, Drina. How glad I am to see you so much recovered. For the first two days, with the doctors looking so grave, I was quite out of my mind with worry. I cancelled all my engagements whilst you were so ill, but Mama wouldn't hear of it once you were out of danger."

"And quite rightly too. Everyone has been so

kind, Louisa, but you had no cause to worry. I have a constitution like a horse."

Louisa giggled. "No wonder you have fitted in so well with Arundale's life."

She smiled weakly at her cousin's joke and then Louisa seated herself on a chair near to the sofa so that they could converse more easily. "Mama sends you her love. She will call in by and by, but you know she has a fear of sick-rooms, Drina."

"Yes, I recall."

She studied her cousin for a moment or two. She looked delightful in her pink bonnet and pelisse, both edged with soft white fur. She was quite different in looks to Lady Petley, but equally as ravishing, which made Drina feel more inferior than ever. Louisa's cheeks were pink too, indicating that the cold snap was continuing.

"I do hope there is no snow next week when we go to Suffolk," Louisa began.

"I agree, for I do not relish a journey on ice-packed roads. But let us talk of other things, dearest. In six weeks—less now!—you will be married."

Louisa, to Drina's surprise, looked far from heartened at the reminder, and her cousin was dismayed. "Louisa, there is nothing wrong is there? Harborough . . ."

"Oh, no," she hastened to assure her, "nothing at all. Harborough would as lief bring forward the marriage if he could. That is the trouble . . ."

Drina sat up, alert at this, and she allowed the rug covering her legs to fall to the floor. "Trouble! Louisa, you must tell me what it is. You haven't had a change of heart, have you?"

The girl shook her head. "No! Never, Drina. It is only . . ." She looked up quickly and then away again. "You recall on the night of your rout that I asked if I may call on you the very next day. . . ."

"Why, yes, I do."

"When I did call you were too ill to see me."

"Then you must delay no longer; tell me now."

Louisa began to pick at the fur of her muff. "I have asked Mama, but she says it will be time enough for me to know once I am married, and then I recalled how often we used to talk, oh, about so many things . . ."

"Louisa," her cousin said in a patient voice, "what is it you wish to talk about?"

At this Louisa rushed across to her and knelt down by the sofa. "Drina, I am so *afraid*. You must tell me what I am to do, for I do so want to make him happy. There is no one else I can ask, and after all you are so recently wed yourself. You must help me, for I am so desperate."

At last she did understand, and she laid her head back on the velvet cushion. "Oh, my dear," she murmured. She was tempted to laugh at the very irony of the situation.

"Help me, Drina," Louisa pleaded, her blue eyes filling with tears. "I do not know of anyone else I can go to."

"Really, my love, you are getting into a pucker over nothing." Drina raised her cousin's chin so that they could look at each other. "Do you love Harborough?"

"So very much, Drina. You couldn't imagine . . ."

She smiled faintly. "Then you will make him happy, my dear, have no fear of that. But your Mama is right, I must own. There is nothing more I can say to you."

The girl's eyes filled with dismay. "But, Drina . . ."

She turned away so that her cousin could not see the tears which had sprung to her eyes. "Please, Louisa, ask no more, I beg of you."

"I have tired you!" she cried. "Oh, Drina, I am so sorry. I am a thoughtless, selfish creature, and I hate myself."

At this the Countess smiled at her, blinking back the tears. "No, I am quite recovered now." She patted her hand. "Louisa, my love, you are going to be very happily married. I know it."

The girl beamed. "Yes, you are right and I am a silly goose. Harborough is the sweetest, kindest man I have ever known, and he adores me. What more could I ask?

"And even though Arundale didn't really

want to marry you initially, you have made him happy too, so you must be correct. Everyone remarks on the change in his character."

"Do they?" Drina asked in a small voice, turning her face away again.

It seemed that everyone had succeeded in forgetting the circumstances of their marriage, except for the Earl and Drina herself. Once more she was near to tears and she could only assume her own low state to blame for this. She was not normally so weak-minded.

Louisa got to her feet. "I *have* tired you, so I shall go now and return on the morrow."

"No!" Drina said quickly, and then smiling, "Tell me, has Miss Peters called on you yet? I instructed her to do so without delay."

Louisa was easily diverted. She sat down again. "She is making the most delightful gowns for me, Drina. One is in pink satin, embroidered with little beads. Oh, and yesterday Mama bought a length of the most adorable white sarsnet. Of course, I did show you the swansdown which is for the velvet evening dress. Miss Peters has the most delightful design for it. Papa says this wedding will send him to the Jews!"

Drina sank back into the cushions, eager to hear her cousin's idle chatter which came as a welcome change from the dark thoughts so often prevalent in her mind these days.

SIX

THE journey to Arundale Park was quite different to the one undertaken immediately after Drina's wedding. For one thing, she was far less apprehensive this time, and on this occasion she did not feel strange in the company of the Earl or feel bound to offer idle conversation to him as he sat opposite to her in the carriage reading a book.

Because of her recent illness he had taken care to instruct the lackeys to ensure that her ladyship was warmly wrapped and that a hot brick was placed at her feet. He had gone so far as to fetch an extra fur rug to place over her knees himself before they had started out on this journey.

Whilst Drina revelled in any attention he bestowed on her and was grateful for it, her heart was still heavy. She could not even dislike Lady Petley and she could not grow accustomed to the ways of the *ton* despite the fact she had been a part of it for some months now.

As the carriage jolted over frozen ruts in the road he glanced up at her and remarked, "We shall be in Cambridge in time for dinner."

She smiled. "I hope it is as good a dinner as on the last occasion, for I am already hungry. Isn't that odd? I had a perfectly good breakfast this morning."

"It is a good sign. You need to eat well now, my dear. You have grown thinner since you were ill."

"When we lived in Lincolnshire I had an enormous appetite, so I don't doubt the good Suffolk air will work as well."

He watched her curiously for a moment or two. "You are obviously looking forward to our time in the country."

Drina recalled her first view of Arundale Park all those months ago. How overawed she had been of that mansion, so large, so different to Rington Manor. She did look forward to returning now, mainly because she suspected it was her husband's favourite home. Built of pale-grey stone, the Palladian-style mansion, with its ornate gardens and a treasure house of precious paintings, was a place of which any-one would be proud.

"Very much," she answered at last. "When we were first married I was glad to hide there for a while to grow accustomed to the change in my status."

"With so many people arriving it will not be restful on this occasion." He frowned. "I wish you had allowed me to cancel it, Drina. Everyone would have understood the reason."

"And everyone, including myself, is anticipating the houseparty with great pleasure. It would have been a pity to disappoint them. And there has been little for me to do except allocate the rooms. Your servants are well trained."

"Well, I don't wish you to overtax yourself. It would be most unwise at this time."

She warmed to his concern however perfunctory it may be. "By the by, Simon, I did invite Mr Fine as you asked, and he was glad to accept. He called in to tell me so himself. He's an odd man. I really don't know what to make of him, although one cannot fault his manner."

The Earl considered for a moment. "Yes, I too find him something of an enigma. I cannot say I fully like the man although he is well conversant with all topics of importance and, as you say, his manner is exemplary. He shows such an interest in horseracing I couldn't fail to invite him, especially as he has purchased such a fine beast. Perhaps it is simply a natural suspicion of anyone who might be *noveau riche*."

Drina chuckled softly. "Does that include *me*, Simon?" she asked mischievously.

His face relaxed as he gazed at her and she found her cheeks flooding with colour. "I think that everything has worked out very well indeed," he said after a moment. "Much better than anyone could have hoped in the circumstances."

She flicked through the pages of her magazine. "I cannot help but feel, though, that you could never forget those circumstances."

As she glanced at him half-fearfully, he was gazing at her still, but his eyes were hard now. "And I feel, Drina, that it is you who finds it difficult to forget."

The carriage jerked and the Earl peered out of the window. "Ah, we have arrived at the inn already." He smiled at her blandly. "You shall have your dinner, and sooner than we thought."

As the lackey pulled down the steps and the Earl stepped down, giving her his hand, she was suddenly reminded of the anger he had displayed when Hugo had tried to kiss her the other evening. In a flight of fancy she could almost imagine it to be jealousy if she hadn't known better.

He was looking up at her, his expression as

bland and disinterested as ever. Her eyes met his and a quiver of excitement shot through her entire being and it was as if time itself had stood still.

"Drina?"

She quickly collected her muff and then, sighing with resignation, she sat forward and reached for his hand.

As Drina had stated, the Earl's servants were well trained, and on her arrival at Arundale Park she found all was in readiness for their guests. After inspecting all the rooms put into use and ascertaining that the amount and type of food necessary had been brought in, Drina was able to report favourably to her husband.

"Our guests may arrive as soon as they please," she told him over breakfast two days after they had arrived.

Sharing any meal with him except for dinner was a novelty, for he was most usually up and abroad long before Drina, who still found the social round a mite hectic. Seeing him at any time was a pleasure, and knowing this was more likely during a sojourn in the country could only enhance her liking for the Earl's country estate.

He glanced at her over his coffee cup and smiled. "These past two days must have been hectic for you, but you do look much better already. The pallor in your cheeks has gone."

Drina flushed slightly at his words, for he could not possibly know what one word of praise or flattery from his lips could do to her.

"We are," he went on moments later, "gaining quite a handsome reputation for our entertaining. Did you know?"

"I couldn't fail to know it, and I am glad I have not failed you, Simon," she murmured as she sipped at her coffee.

Drina was only too well aware that many a brilliant society hostess was born of a loveless marriage. Louisa, for instance, would find enough fulfilment in her marriage to suffice with the occasional rout or card party.

As he finished his breakfast she said, "Are you going over to the stables again today?"

"Of course." He folded his copy of *The Times* which he had been reading and glanced at her. After hesitating a moment, he said, "If everything is in readiness and you are not needed here, why don't you come with me this morning? If you feel well enough, naturally."

"Yes, indeed," she answered, trying to suppress the excitement bubbling up inside her, "I am well enough. Please do not think I am a delicate female, for I am not in the least."

His smile was an indulgent one, which reminded Drina of that which an older brother might bestow on the little sister who amused him.

"I think you tend to be negligent of yourself, Drina. I seem to recall a day when you wore wet slippers." Her cheeks flushed at the reminder of her distress on that occasion. "Braving the February night clad in nothing but a thin gown is sufficient to lay low the most healthy female, and I must ask you to take more care in the future."

"If it matters to you, Simon," she answered, lowering her eyes demurely, "I shall certainly do so."

Abruptly the Earl pushed back his chair and got to his feet. "Naturally, it matters to me. I shall have a gig brought round while you change your clothes."

With the help of Hollis, the abigail engaged for her on her marriage, Drina was soon changed into her riding outfit. She often rode in Rotten Row to receive the admiration of many of the bucks promenading there in the afternoon. Sometimes she was accompanied by Louisa or a group of her friends and often Lady Petley came with her on those rides, and they made a handsome pair, riding their thoroughbreds or driving in Arundale's high perch phaeton. Belatedly, Drina recalled as she hurried down the great staircase pulling on her gloves, that it was Hélène who had chosen this riding habit for her.

"The dark blue, Drina," she had said. "It is the perfect colour for you, *ma chère*."

The Earl was waiting by the gig and as he conversed with the groom he was slapping his riding whip against his thighs with scarce concealed impatience. Drina paused on the top step, gazing down at him, determined that for today at least she would put all thoughts of Hélène's relationship with her husband from her mind and enjoy his company. He looked up to see her standing there. He raised his whip in acknowledgment of her presence and as she hurried forward to join him she told herself she had so much more than she ever dreamed possible. It was selfish to wish for more.

The stables which were sited on the Earl's land some way from the house but adjacent to the Heath, were almost as magnificent as Arundale Park itself. Drina found that they were far larger than she had imagined and that no expense had been spared for the horses' comfort and well-being. It was only when she noted the bewildering number of horses there that she fully realised the Earl's commitment to racing.

Mr Potts, the Earl's head groom and trainer, who was responsible for the success of the horses on the track, escorted them on a tour of the stalls. Drina exclaimed often at such a collection of thoroughbreds, many of which were hooded and heavily blanketed, indicating that they were in intense training.

"Which is to be raced in the Kelvington Plate?" she asked, becoming interested despite her ignorance.

"It was to have been Marmina, but Potts tells me she has strained a forelock on the gallop yesterday, so it will have to be . . ." he glanced at the head groom and added, "Athena."

"Will she be ready?"

The Earl allowed her to peep into the stall where the filly was hooded and blanketed so it would be sweated in preparation for the big race.

"She will be in the peak of condition by the great day," the Earl observed. "Come along this way; I have something which might interest you far more."

The object of interest was a foal, newly born, which delighted Drina, and she crooned over him for some few minutes under the Earl's indulgent eye and the mare's more suspicious one. As Drina delighted over the small creature, becoming covered in hay in the process, the Earl ran his hand along the mare's flank.

"Juno was a great racer in her day. If her foal is half as good I shall be satisfied."

Drina straightened up at last. "It will be so exciting watching her race eventually, having seen her so small."

The Earl's eyes twinkled with amusement.

"There will be many more for you to follow. At the moment three others are in foal."

There came the sound of hooves in the courtyard and the Earl tapped her arm with his whip. "D'you fancy a ride along the gallop, Drina?"

She followed him out of the stall. "Can you trust me on one of those animals? They are so very precious."

He looked at her in surprise, brushing away a piece of hay which had adhered to her back. "Why do you malign yourself so? You have a fine seat."

She flushed again. "Louisa always admired my riding skill, but that is of no account."

He was gazing at her thoughtfully. "Your cousin admires you greatly."

She bit her lip, recalling her inability to help her cousin the last time they had met. That omission still jarred and would, Drina thought, continue to do so. It was the very first time she had been forced to turn away from Louisa.

"I am very fond of her," she answered, and when he made no further comment but simply went on gazing at her she continued, "She never alluded to my position in their household. We have always been as sisters."

"It is fortunate she will remain in London after her marriage. She will be a true companion for you."

"It will be good to have her near," Drina answered warmly.

"Kharma will suit her ladyship, my lord," Potts said, leading the filly towards her.

When she hesitated, the Earl's eyebrows rose a fraction. "Have you changed your mind about accompanying us?"

"I do not wish to displace a groom. It would not be fair."

He threw back his head and laughed. "Oh, my dear, the groom will not mind at all if you displace him on this occasion, or any other for that matter. Riding can become a chore when it is part of one's obligations."

As she went towards the mounting block the Earl caught her arm and she looked at him questioningly. "Drina, before our guests arrive I would like to make a request of you."

"Of course."

"Francis is worried about Hélène. You may have noticed she is not quite herself of late. She is still a stranger and possibly unhappy about her past experiences, which, Francis tells me, were not at all pleasant." He looked away. "We may only guess at them, of course."

"What is it you want of me?" she asked, her voice stiff and not quite steady.

"I would be obliged if you would go out of your way to accommodate her. She is of a nervous disposition."

Drina continued to look at him steadily as he

spoke and his gaze did not flicker. He could not possibly have guessed by her calm stance the familiar lump which had formed in her throat and threatened to choke her. There was nothing she could do, no way in which to fight for his love. She could not accuse him even of indiscretion, and even if she could she would not find it in her heart to do so.

Unable to speak at all, she merely nodded, and then turned to where the groom was waiting with the horse.

Drina returned alone to Arundale Park after her ride on the gallop. It had been invigorating riding at speed on such a swift mount even though the condition of the ground was far from perfect. There had been a hard frost which rendered the ground too firm, but not being an expert of any kind on horse racing, Drina had enjoyed riding behind the Earl who was mounted on yet another of his splendid beasts. He was a fine rider, which she had noted before, having a great accord with his mount. As he galloped along he looked carefree and happier than at any time she had seen him before.

He would, she knew, spend the remainder of the day at the stables, the place in which he was happiest, so after returning the horses to their stalls, Drina took her leave of him and returned to the house in the gig. He would discuss feeding methods with his trainer and pore over the accounts, and there was no way in which Drina could join him, much to her regret.

To her surprise, as they approached the house a carriage stood in front of it. As she was helped down from the gig she gazed at it curiously. It was rather old-fashioned but luxurious nevertheless, and at that moment a preponderance of luggage was being unloaded and carried up the steps by the footmen.

The first of their guests were not expected for another day, so it was with a great deal of curiosity that Drina hurried up the steps. The butler immediately appeared and it seemed he had lost little of his calm.

"Who is here?" she demanded.

"The Dowager Countess, m'lady."

Drina's eyes grew large with fright. Simon's grandmother! In the three months since her marriage she had heard so much about this old woman, and none of it was reassuring. For a long time now she had dreaded the time that they would have to visit Cheltenham, but now the old lady was here! She put one hand to her head in bewilderment. If only Simon were here.

"The Dowager Countess is in the blue drawing-room, my lady, and I have taken the liberty of having her ladyship's luggage taken up to her customary suite in the south wing."

"That is quite in order," she answered abstractedly, and then, as she moved away from him, "Have a message taken to his lordship, Carter. He's at the stables."

She ran up the stairs in a most unladylike way, calling frantically for her maid. By the time the girl rushed into the room, breathless too and full of apologies, Drina was already stepping out of her riding habit.

"What shall I wear, Hollis? I fear it makes no odds. The blue sprigged muslin . . . no, the grey gingham is more demure. What *shall* I say to her, Hollis? I fear I shall be tongue-tied."

The girl clucked her tongue as she fastened the gown in a manner that seemed to be maddeningly slow. "You will contrive, m'lady. Have no fear about that. Most of the other servants were here in the days gone by, so's she can't be so bad, can she?"

"From what I have heard, Hollis, she is far worse!"

Her hands were trembling too as she attempted to comb her curls which had become somewhat disarrayed under her jaunty riding hat.

The abigail clasped a string of pearls around her mistress's neck. "Take a deep breath, m'lady, like you always do before you go downstairs to greet anyone, and you'll be equal to her, I guarantee."

When she entered the blue drawing-room a few minutes later little of her nervousness was apparent. The Dowager Countess was being wrapped in a shawl and a rug when Drina first clapped eyes on her. She had expected to see an old lady, but not one quite as old as this. There seemed to be a million wrinkles on her face and, clad in black from head to toe, she presented an alarming sight to one already almost out of her mind with fright.

"Lady Arundale," she said in a soft voice.

The companion who was so busily settling her mistress paused to bob a deep curtsey, eyeing her curiously at the same time. The Dowager's eyes were no more than two further wrinkles as she peered across the room.

"Come closer," she snapped. "How in heaven's name can you expect me to see you if you remain at the other side of the room?"

Drina's impulse was to dash forward to obey her, but instead she forced herself to walk across the room slowly, noting that the bony hand which clutched an ebony stick glittered with jewellery. The companion's eyes gleamed too, with anticipation. In her place Drina would also anticipate an interesting meeting.

"Rowlands, you may leave us," the old woman commanded. "See that the maids are unpacking my things properly and that nothing is broken or crushed. You know how clumsy those creatures can be if they are not supervised properly."

The companion's face registered dismay for

one moment and then, recovering herself, she curtseyed and left the room.

"Dratted woman," complained the Dowager. "Pity an old woman forced to rely on her kind offices."

Drina could not imagine anyone who was less in need of pity.

"We did not look to see you here at this time, your ladyship," she managed at last, "so this is quite a surprise."

The old lady turned that disconcerting stare on her again. "A pleasant one, I trust."

"Naturally." The old woman wheezed, rocking back and forth slightly in her chair. "But we did not have notice of your coming."

"Wasn't sure I would make it."

"May I ring for some refreshment?" Drina asked, going towards the bell-pull.

"Just want a coze with my new grand-daughter, that's all." As Drina came back towards her she said, "Well, let me look at you." She did so. "So," she said after what seemed to be a great length of time, "you are the minx who tricked my grandson into marriage."

Drina gasped. "That is untrue. Totally untrue. I did no such thing. It was an accident."

The old lady chuckled, delighted at her indignation, patting the seat at her side. "Sit down, sit down, will you, before I get a crick in my neck from looking up at you."

Drina obeyed without thinking. "Didn't you *know* about our marriage?"

"I know everything about m'grandson. Make it my business to, although I know more about horses. I must own, however, I haven't heard a jot of gossip about you since you wed, and that's to your credit, my girl."

Drina took another deep breath before replying, "I am gratified, your ladyship."

"How is Simon? Is he well?"

"Very well."

"I'm glad to hear it." She peered disconcertingly at Drina again. "Knew your grandfather many years ago." Drina's face brightened, and then the Dowager scowled, "Never liked the fellow."

Drina's head fell back on to the sofa. Oh, she prayed silently, someone please come soon and rescue me.

"You must know about Fenella Goodmaye, I suppose?"

Drina raised her head and her eyes widened. "The name is not familiar, my lady."

"So you don't," she said with some satisfaction. "Simon was going to marry her. It must have been about ten years ago now. My, how time does go when one is growing old."

Her heart sank. "Yes, I have heard he was very much in love with someone," she answered in a muted voice.

"Bah, love. That spineless chit. Ran off with

an officer in the Dragoons three weeks before the wedding. Just as well. Foolish chit to give up the name of Arundale to follow the drum. Wouldn't have done for Simon, though. Knew it all the time. She would have had sickly babies. No doubt of that. Suppose *you* will think it romantic."

"No," Drina answered, feeling slightly faint, "quite the contrary. I told Simon about my parents—it was a similar story, I fear. It must have caused him great pain."

"In his pride. That hurt him most of all. Namby-pamby creature. Never did approve."

She placed one bony hand on Drina's knee. "This could have turned out worse. You look healthy enough."

"I am," she answered uncertainly.

"You are married to him and what's done can't be undone, and you can fill this mausoleum with children; lots of 'em."

Drina stared at her in horror, but the old lady seemed unaware of it. "Told Simon at the time you were married, I haven't lost hope of seeing my great-grandson—not yet!" She laughed gruffly. "But you'd better not be long about it."

Drina was choked with an anger she couldn't possibly express. The Dowager was every bit as horrific as she had been led to believe.

To her relief at that moment the door burst open and Simon marched in.

"Grandmama! What on earth brings you here?"

"What a welcome. I thought you might be glad to see me."

He kissed her. "I'm delighted to see you," he said, and Drina didn't doubt it was true. There was an affinity between the two which was hard to understand. He gave Drina a reassuring smile which did nothing to alleviate the mortification his grandmother's words had caused her. "But it must be unwise for you to travel at this time of the year," he added in a severe tone.

"Did you think I would miss the Kelvington Plate? What are you racing this year?"

"Athena."

She nodded sagely. "A promising filly, if I recall correctly. You will have to watch Boynton, though. His jockey'll unseat yours if he can."

"Froggett is equal to any trick from that quarter, Grandmama, never you fear."

Striving hard to conceal her relief Drina got to her feet. "If you will both excuse me, I have a great deal to do before dinner."

"Good!" the Dowager exclaimed. "Off you go then. Want to talk to m'grandson."

She winked conspiratorially at Drina who was horrified, but she had no cause to do anything other than curtsey and leave them together.

SEVEN

DRINA was still angry when they sat down to dinner. The unfortunate Miss Rowlands spoke only when addressed, and as the Dowager and her grandson continued their discussion about horses during the meal, the young Countess's mood did not improve. Fortunately, the Dowager tired easily and went to her room early, so that Drina was spared any further intimate conversations that the old lady might demand—at least for that day. She trembled to think of all those which could follow, for it was certain, having endured the ordeal of such a long journey, the Dowager would remain at her ancestral home for some considerable time to come.

It was odd that, having charmed some of the most fearsome leaders of the *ton*, Drina had been totally unnerved by one very old lady. But the thought of her remaining there, seeing everything and knowing all, could scarce be borne.

After the Dowager had retired and Miss Rowlands with her, the Earl went to the library to his books, and Drina consoled herself with a last-minute inspection of the guest bedrooms. She was weary by the time she reached her own room—it was obvious the illness had taken a greater toll of her strength than she believed—but by the time Hollis had left her she was wide awake and settled down by the fire to read a book. The story was a lurid one, chosen for her by Louisa, and not to Drina's taste at all, so she found it difficult to concentrate. Her mind, inevitably, kept returning to her meeting with the Earl's grandmother. The Dowager's voice kept coming between her and the page, making her angry again, and the anger grew once more until she could no longer sit at all.

She began to pace the floor, clasping and unclasping her hands until her own agitation became almost too much to bear, but when she heard the sound of voices in the room next to hers she stopped her pacing. There was a communicating door between their rooms; it was never locked, but neither of them had ever opened it. Now she hesitated, and after a moment or two went through into the Earl's room where he was being helped out of his coat by his valet. Both men looked surprised to see her, as well they might.

"Is anything amiss, Drina?" asked the Earl.

"May I speak to you?" she said in a breathless voice, striving to appear calm. She was most anxious not to allow her inner anger and anxiety to be evident to her husband.

"It is hardly the hour for discussion."

"Please, Simon!"

The Earl glanced at his valet. "That will be all for tonight, Sawkins. Don't bother to wait up any longer."

"As you wish, m'lord."

As the servant left the room the Earl said, "Surely this could have waited until tomorrow."

"Tomorrow there will be no opportunity," she said in a suddenly bitter voice. "You will go to the stud farm and I shall be engaged with our visitors as they arrive."

He sank down on the edge of the bed and began to remove his neckcloth whilst Drina watched him, feeling less and less certain of herself and certainly more and more angry. She clasped her hands in front of her in an effort to stop them trembling.

"Your grandmother . . ." she began.

He glanced up at her. "Grandmama is well

pleased with you, which is no small achievement."

"Oh, Simon, she hates me!"

"Nonsense," he answered briskly, when it was really sympathy she required at that moment. "I assure you she is impressed by your bearing."

"How can she be? Her only grandson married against his will to a girl of low origins and no fortune."

His smile was one of infinite patience. "You may have had no fortune, although that was hardly of any importance to me anyway, but you are certainly not of low origins."

She turned away from him in an agony of frustration. "You know what I mean. In other circumstances you would never have chosen me."

He drew a deep sigh. "There is no point in discussing that now, Drina. Now, don't get into a pucker over this. Grandmama is alarming, I grant you, but we must indulge her. She is a very old lady."

"I trust she will be returning to her home soon," she said, turning to face him anxiously again.

"I doubt it. I don't think you realise what an effort and an ordeal it has been for her to come here."

"It is only because she wishes to inspect me."

"That is quite natural. I am her only grandson and my welfare must be of the utmost importance to her."

"Your welfare!" Drina's anger was returning now. "She is a horrid old woman and I shall not tolerate her here to interfere in my life!"

The Earl got to his feet, no longer so amiable or conciliatory. "Drina, it is her home, you will recall."

There was no mistaking the resolve in his voice, and Drina was once more reminded that although he had always been equable to all she had done, deep inside him there still remained a hard core of resentment, but she felt goaded beyond all caution now. Suddenly, from all seeming rosy she felt alone and friendless, and the isolation was a fearful thing.

"For good or ill it is *my* home too. Oh, I know you have been kind to me since our wedding and I have wanted for nothing, but that doesn't mean I must endure insults even if it is from your grandmother."

"She appears to insult everyone, Drina, but in reality it is nothing of the sort. She belongs to a less fastidious age; it is nothing."

"To you perhaps," she went on indignantly, "but I refuse, absolutely refuse—do you hear?—to be treated as no better than a . . . brood mare in your stud farm!"

He stared at her in astonishment for a moment or two, and then to her further dismay he began to laugh. "My God! When have I ever treated you so, you silly goose?"

"Not you!" she blazed. "It is worse because it is her!"

He was still laughing at her, which did nothing to quell her anger. "Anyone less like a horse I have never seen," he went on. "You are very much a woman."

"That old harridan," she fumed, stamping her foot on the floor. "I was never more humiliated in my whole life. She *is* a witch . . ."

Taking two strides, he had crossed the room and dealt her a ringing blow across one cheek. Drina gasped mid-sentence and clasped her hand to her cheek, biting back her tears.

"Let us be plain, madam," he said in a hard voice which cut her like a knife. "That old witch as you call her has cared for me since I was five years old, and I love her more dearly than anyone else alive. I will not have you or anyone else haranging her. You will treat her with the respect her age and position demand. Do you understand?"

She looked fearfully into his face, uncompromisingly grim, and nodded. She ran back into her own room, sinking down on to the bed. She gulped back her tears, feeling, so deep was her misery, that she could drown in it.

A moment later a footstep on the floor beside the bed caused her to look up fearfully.

"I apologise," he said in a soft voice. All his anger was gone.

"I . . . am sorry . . . too," she gulped. "It was . . . wrong of me . . . to speak as I did."

He went across the room and returned a moment later, having rung out his handkerchief in water. As he sat down beside her she allowed him to raise her head and put the blessed coolness of the handkerchief against her cheek.

"There," he said, "I doubt if you will be scarred at all."

She laughed nervously. "As if anyone would care if I were."

"I would care," he said in some surprise. "It is very gratifying to have one's wife the centre of admiration."

She stared at him for a long moment in astonishment and then slowly he bent his head and kissed her very gently on the lips. Immediately all her anger and resentment against him was gone and only the wonder of a great and miraculous discovery took its place. As brief as it was, the kiss served to show her that his love would, indeed, be a wonderful thing, if only it hadn't been destroyed by that beauty all those years ago.

"My grandmother," he went on a moment later when he drew away, "is wiser than we would credit her, Drina. There is much sense in what she says—always. She sees us as successfully married, and I begin to think that we are. This mariage of ours, however contracted, has not turned out ill, you must own."

"It has been a very great thing for me," she answered in a quiet voice. The feel of his lips was still evident on hers and it filled her with a sense of awe.

"And when one glances around it is obvious we are happier than most. . . ."

It was Drina who pulled away from him at last. "What exactly is it you are trying to say to me, Simon?"

He stared down at the floor. "It would grieve me if the line were to die out after I am gone."

She drew in a sharp breath. "You never used to care."

He gazed at her. "I do now."

"Because it is what your grandmother wishes."

He looked surprised. "I suppose she would be pleased if I were to have an heir."

"You look as if she has not discussed it with you," Drina said in a quiet voice.

"She has not mentioned it to me since before we were married."

"Well, she has certainly mentioned it to me."

There was a brief silence before he began to laugh again. "So now I understand all that indignation." She flashed him a furious glance and he looked regretful. "I am sorry, Drina; she can be confoundedly tactless. You must realise this has nothing to do with Grandmama. I am growing older and there seems no reason to allow my estates to pass to another branch of the family if it is not necessary. You must agree that this is sense."

"Yes." Her voice was barely audible.

"Perhaps you would give the matter your consideration...."

Drina laughed mirthlessly. "And if I refuse? What will you do then?"

"I shall be disappointed and hope one day you will change your mind, but I will of course respect any decision that you make."

Suddenly she could not stop the tears any more and they began to roll down her cheeks. It was all so cold and calculating, so far removed from what she wanted and the hope she had harboured that one day he would look at her and realise he loved her. How impossible a dream that was; he had long ago forgotten what it was to love at all.

He raised her chin with his finger. "I am sorry, Drina. I did not mean to distress you. I wouldn't want to do anything to put you out of countenance. Surely you must know that."

She shook her head, brushing away the tears as she did so. "You have been most considerate in every way, Simon, and it is not you who has caused me to weep. I am a foolish creature, for I was just recalling my last conversation with

Louisa." He was watching her curiously, so very near to her. She made a sound, half laughter, half sobbing. "With her wedding only a few weeks hence, she came to me for advice. Naturally, I could not help her at all."

His arm was around her shoulders, drawing her even closer, making her breathless. "Your cousin will be here tomorrow, so there is still time."

She looked up into his face for a long moment and then his lips brushed the cheek which no longer hurt her. Drina closed her eyes and his lips met hers once more. She could envisage Lady Petley in his arms, not immobile like herself, but full of all the love she had to give to him. She pushed the image further away. Hélène did not matter, could not matter—not tonight anyway. . . .

By mid-morning the house was a hive of activity. For once Drina would have given much to have had the place to herself and the Earl too, but as carriage followed carriage relentlessly along the tree-lined drive, she recognised that this wish could not come true for some time. At least, she acknowledged, with so many persons present there was less chance of being thrown into the Dowager's company. The old lady herself seemed perfectly content to renew old acquaintances and to enquire into the antecedents of others.

Most of the visiting gentlemen were immediately whisked off to the racing stables to watch the horses being exercised, and the ladies were left to discuss the latest fashions and scandal until it was time to dress for dinner.

Just as Drina was about to go down to their guests the Earl came into her room. This was only the second time he had entered her bedroom and she felt as embarrassed as if they had just met.

"Oh, Simon," she gasped, going on to say the first thing which came into her mind, "I was just wondering which jewels I should wear tonight. Which do you think would be best?"

"The diamonds," he said without hesitation.

"But I have no . . ."

Before she could finish he had produced a glittering necklace, the famous Arundale diamonds she had heard to much about.

"Grandmama wishes you to have them now."

Drina found she was too choked to speak as he clasped them about her throat. They glittered and reflected a thousand lights from the candelabrum and she stared at their incredible beauty which felt cold against her throat.

After a moment she said in a small voice, "I am most obliged to her."

"Grandmama obviously realises they would become you far better, as of course they do."

"You are very gallant," she answered, trembling beneath the hand that remained on her shoulder.

She longed to turn and throw her arms about him and admit her love for him, but sadly she knew she would only cause him to shrink from her, and so she remained silent.

A moment later he was opening the door, bowing low and making a sweeping gesture with his arm. "To our guests, Drina. It would not do for any of them to be downstairs before us."

After dinner, the gentlemen and quite a number of the ladies sat down to whist and faro, staking quite frightening amounts of money. Drina had never grown accustomed to the staggering amounts of money won and lost at card games. Louisa's forthcoming nuptuals was the main topic of conversation amongst the ladies, whilst the race meeting about to be held took pride of place amongst the gentlemen. Drina realised, belatedly, that she would have to, in the future, take a great deal of interest in this passion of her husband.

She had noticed also, in the course of the day, that Lady Petley was in a very despondent state of mind, although she was striving hard to hide it behind a gay smile when anyone conversed with her. Drina felt she knew her better than to be deceived by it even if the others were, and if she were not so afraid of what she might discover by so doing Drina would have sought to gain her confidence. As matters stood she could only wait helplessly, torn apart by her own doubts and jealousies. Now she knew, selfish as it seemed, nothing would suffice but to be the only woman in the Earl's life, and that was an impossible wish.

"Simon," said Sir Francis, his voice a whisper, "have you had a chance to observe Hélène since we arrived?"

The Earl averted his gaze from the card table at which he had been a spectator for the last few minutes and he looked round at his friend.

"She is as lovely as ever, that much I have noted."

"I caught her burning a note the other day and then she declared she didn't want to come here. I couldn't understand it; she's so fond of the Countess."

"Perhaps she doesn't like race meetings, Francis. We never stop to think that they can be dev'lishly boring for the ladies."

The young man looked wretched. "And it might be because she is unhappy with me. Perhaps there is someone else after all."

"She is devoted to you, Francis. I would stake any amount on that."

His friend smiled grimly. "I wonder what kind of odds would be staked on it in St James's."

"Oh, come now, Francis, this is quite unlike you."

"Her moods are so uncertain. . . . She's as melancholy as a gib-cat."

The Earl laughed. "Show me a woman who isn't dev'lish flighty in her moods."

"Your wife for one, Simon. I have never known another woman so even-tempered as the Countess. Nothing puts her into a pucker."

The Earl had to agree, although, recalling the quick flashes of temper he sometimes witnessed, this was not strictly true, especially last night when her anger had angered and excited him so. He had never seen her look so . . . lovely. She was almost beautiful when the colour came to her cheeks and her eyes grew bright with defiance. How he regretted that momentary impulse which made him hurt her. That look on her face when he had slapped her would remain in his memory for ever, and it had happened all because he had suddenly realised that she was a woman, and one more fetching than any he had ever seen before.

"Simon." His friend's whisper broke into his thoughts most welcomingly. "I've been wondering if you weren't right about caution." The Earl looked perplexed. "I didn't care about the life she might have led before we met—still don't, for that matter—but what if . . . there is insanity in the family? Didn't think of that, but it could explain a great deal."

Suddenly the Earl exploded into laughter. "Don't even think of it, Francis. Lady Petley is a fine woman and there is nothing wrong with her that time will not put right. As I have said, dev'lish uncertain the humours of women." He glanced across the room. "Say no more about it, my friend, for I do believe Mr Fine is approaching us."

Sir Francis scowled. "I don't like that man. Caught him being familiar with m'wife once, although Hélène denied any impropriety."

"You see too much where Lady Petley is concerned."

Mr Augustus Fine smiled confidently at the two men and seemed unaware that Sir Francis was glowering at him.

"What d'you think of Rondel, your lordship?"

"A fine beast," the Earl answered as Sir Francis took a recently vacated seat at the card table. "You will be the envy of many men when you race him."

"I am most obliged to you for accepting him into your stables."

The Earl smiled. "There is always room for so fine a beast in my stables, Mr Fine, as I believe you must know. It came as a surprise to everyone when you bid so high for him."

The man smiled with satisfaction. "When I do anything, Lord Arundale, I do it thoroughly."

"A man after my own heart," the Earl answered.

Mr Augustus Fine smiled again, bowed low and walked towards Lady Petley. The Earl watched him and as he did so a faint suspicion crossed his mind. Lady Petley and Mr Fine. Could that be the answer? It seemed unthinkable, a lady so lovely and having so dashing a husband. Mr Fine would be almost fifty, and plump, hardly a ladies' man for all his fine manners. Lord Arundale was disturbed once more by his friend's unhappiness, but after the fiasco at Southways he was more than ever determined to remain aloof from it.

It was some time later that he was accosted yet again, this time by Lady Petley herself. She laid her hand on his arm and led him smilingly towards the Conservatory.

"Tell me, Lord Arundale," she said in a conversational tone which betrayed nothing of her unease, "do you think the course will be suitable for the race tomorrow?"

The Earl glanced at her in surprise. "A trifle hard perhaps, but not impossible." After a pause he went on, "I had no idea you were so interested in horseracing, Lady Petley."

She laughed softly. "I know little about anything, you must own, and Francis is so interested and knowledgeable I must learn as much as I can."

"I am sure he would be as happy as I am to assist you."

"It is strange, is it not, that the Prince of Wales is not present for so important a race as the Kelvington Plate, especially as so many of his friends are here?"

"The Prince rarely attends meetings at Newmarket nowadays, Lady Petley. You could not know, but once, many years ago, he and his jockey were involved in a . . . difference of opinion with the Stewards of the Jockey Club. Ever since then he has avoided the Newmarket course."

"Ah, so now I understand; I was quite puzzled about it for a while."

"It happened many years ago, long before my association with the turf, but, as no doubt you know, His Highness never forgets a hurt."

They had reached the Conservatory by then and the Earl ushered her to a seat.

"I have been seeking an opportunity to speak to you since we arrived, Lord Arundale," she went on moments later. She was pensive now, the bright smile having gone. The Earl suspected he was about to learn the real reason she had accosted him. "I have been wondering if there is anything amiss with your wife."

The Earl looked alarmed, for this was the last thing he had expected. "Drina? I believe she is perfectly well now. She extends herself too hard for the comfort of our guests, but she will not hear of doing less."

"I did not exactly mean her state of health, Lord Arundale. I am distressed and in such circumstances find it difficult to express myself properly . . ."

"I am all patience, Lady Petley."

She took out a scrap of lace with served as a handkerchief and she rolled it, unconsciously, into a ball between her hands.

"I was only wondering if, perhaps, I had offended Lady Arundale in some way, although I cannot conceive how that could be."

"Neither can I, Lady Petley."

"Of late she has been so cold to me. I am a stupid creature, but I sense such things too easily."

The Earl regarded her with sympathy. "Lady Petley, you must remember she was very ill for many days. She showed interest in no one at that time, not even myself."

"But since, Lord Arundale! There have been so many opportunities, and she did not return any of my calls even though she was seen in Harding Howell's in Pall Mall and she attended Sadler's Wells. And since we have been at Arundale Park, Lady Arundale has scarce exchanged a word with me. I am sure I am being deliberately cut. We were so close, I cannot help but notice it, and feel the loss very deeply."

"I am quite sure there is nothing wrong save for the fact that my wife has to divide her time between all her guests. She has always and still does speak of you with the greatest affection. I know Drina is very grateful too for all the help you have afforded her since our marriage."

She smiled again then. "You are most certainly right, Lord Arundale. I have been a goose in thinking anything amiss, and selfish too to expect Lady Arundale's attention when she is so much in demand. Can you forgive my teasing you about so trifling a matter, my lord?"

She was, the Earl thought yet again, the most entrancing creature when tears sparkled like emeralds in her eyes and her lips trembled. Why, if it were not for . . . He thrust the thought from his mind, saying as gently as he could, "Lady Petley, it is possible to forgive you anything."

To his dismay, her large green eyes filled with unshed tears again. "Oh, if only that were true!" she said in anguish. She got hurriedly to her feet. "Please excuse me, Lord Arundale, I have taken up enough of your valuable time over trivialities."

As she hurried away, almost before he could get to his feet, the Earl stared after the slight figure, shaking his head in bewilderment. She really was the oddest creature and he didn't wonder his friend was perplexed. If she was typical of her race he didn't wonder, either, that England had been at war with them for so many years. The Earl, however, had sufficient intellect to realise this was not so. Something was very wrong with Lady Petley and yet again he hoped for Francis's sake insanity was not the answer.

Drina had seen Lady Petley approach and then walk out of the room arm in arm with her husband. Had the woman been any other present she might not have noted it at all, but she had dreaded such a meeting all day. She too had noted Hélène's downcast countenance and now could not help but notice the radiance of her smile as she conversed with the Earl. After a moment or two, unable to bear it any longer, she excused herself and made to follow.

However, she reached the salon when her flight was halted, maddeningly, by a silver-topped walking stick being waved in her face.

"Oh, Lady Arundale," she gasped, and then smiled at Miss Rowlands who was wearing her customary black bombazine. "Are you quite comfortable in here? Not in a draught?"

"I am quite comfortable, thank you. You look fagged, child. Sit down."

Drina looked alarmed. "I was looking for . . . my aunt."

The Dowager gave a most unladylike snort. "She is in the Conservatory, boring poor Edith Portchester with the magnificence of her daughter's future home. The Portchesters know it better than she ever will." Drina hovered there uncertainly, torn apart by frustration. "Sit down," the Dowager said irritably. "Move, Rowlands."

The companion on being prodded by the stick got to her feet and, drawing a sigh of resignation, Drina sat down. "I believe I shall ascertain that the fire has been made up in your ladyship's room," the companion ventured, half fearfully. Drina was keeping her eye on the open door.

"Well, don't just stand there dithering, woman. Do it!"

As she scuttled off, Drina said rather boldly, "Do you not think you are a little hard on Miss Rowlands?"

"Who are you to tell me how to treat m'own servants?"

"I beg your pardon, ma'am."

"Don't ever beg, child. It doesn't suit your character. I'm too soft with her and that's the truth."

Drina bit back a giggle and the old lady pointed her stick towards the door leading to the drawing-room. "Who's the chit playing the harp as if she were already on her way to heaven?"

Drina bit her lip to suppress another giggle. "Louisa Lythe, Lady Arundale. My cousin."

The old lady sniffed derisively and then turned her dreaded gaze on Drina once more. "*You* are Lady Arundale now, you know. I am Grandmama, and I should be obliged if you would remember that." Before Drina could answer she went on, "I knew the diamonds would become you. Told Simon they would."

"I am most obliged to you for them."

"They would be yours one day, so it may as well be now and give me the pleasure of seeing them."

She began to chuckle, and it was just then that Lady Petley came running out of the Conservatory. She stopped for no one and it was obvious she was distressed. A few moments later the Earl followed and Drina got to her feet, aware now only of him.

"Lady Petley seems distraught," she ventured as he approached.

"Yes, it seems that she is," was all he would say, and then turning to his grandmother, "Well, Grandmama, how are you enjoying our little gathering?"

"Splendidly. Just like old times. I tend to forget what a quiet little backwater Cheltenham can be. This kind of a life is more to my liking."

"But you must take care not to tire yourself."

"I find it hard to admit that I do grow tired easily, so if you will be good enough to give me your arm I shall retire now. I must be fit for tomorrow."

Accordingly the Earl gave her his arm whilst Drina helped her to her feet. They made their way through the drawing-room and it was rather like a royal progress. After the Dowager had gone, leaning heavily on her stick and her grandson's arm, Drina was able to return her attention to what troubled her. She found Lady Petley alone in the music-room, picking out a melancholy tune on the harpsichord. She looked startled and more than a little guilty when Drina came into the room and closed the door.

"Hélène," she began, without preamble, "I could not help but see you come out of the Conservatory. Did Arundale do or say anything to put you out of countenance?"

Her eyes grew wide. "*Mais non, cherie.*"

"But something or someone has," she went on in a gentler voice. "Can you not tell me?"

Lady Petley looked away. "It is nothing. I am merely tired after the journey. You must not concern yourself, but you are very kind to ask."

She quickly got to her feet, hurrying across the room. "I believe I shall retire now. Please give my excuses to everyone."

She was gone, leaving Drina to stare after her. After a moment she sank down on to a seat, staring down into her lap. It was Simon, she realised. Hélène was in love with Simon. What the

Earl felt about Lady Petley Drina dare not even consider, but she was certain only love could cause her to be so happy and then so sad. With Simon she had experienced both extremes.

EIGHT

THE day of the Kelvington Plate dawned bright and cold, and after an early breakfast those gentlemen intimately concerned with the race left to inspect the course and to attend the horse sale to be held in Newmarket.

Some time later a cavalcade of handsomely appointed carriages left Arundale Park for Newmarket Heath where the race was to take place. In Drina's carriage was her cousin, Louisa, the Dowager, and Lady Hélène Petley. The Dowager was almost shrouded in furs to withstand the cold. Simon had begged her not to attend the meeting, but he might just as well have held his tongue for the impression he made on her. Just how stubborn she was Drina only realised when they reached a vantage point on the Heath and the horses were unharnessed and led away; the old Countess had come along especially to witness the big race, but from any vantage point she could not possibly see anything of the race, so weak were her eyes.

The Heath was crowded, attracting gypsies, jugglers, flower sellers, as well as the customary number of bookmakers, touts and spectators, of course. The atmosphere was like that of a carnival and Drina found the excitement of the occasion infectious. Louisa was looking as delicate and as lovely as ever, and today she was wearing a blue velvet pelisse and bonnet which complimented the colour of her eyes, her hands snugly ensconced inside her fur muff. Once the carriage was in position she stood up to gaze all around her, her eyes full of excitement. Drina was warmly clad too in a fur cloak and hood which framed her face charmingly. She was glad to see that her cousin was no longer troubled. One day soon she would tell Louisa she need not be, for when one loved there was no fear.

"Oh, *look*; Mama is in the Duke of Portchester's carriage. Mama!"

She began to wave her muff to attract her mother's attention, until the Dowager banged her stick on the floor of the carriage.

"Sit down, young lady, and remember who and where you are!"

Drina grinned as, subdued, Louisa sank back into her seat whispering, "Drina, I am so afraid of the Countess. She is very alarming."

Drina leaned closer. "Everyone finds her alarming, Louisa, even Arundale, I believe, but she is really rather sweet beneath that crusty exterior. I am growing exceedingly fond of her."

Louisa chuckled and she remained silent for only a moment or two. "I saw Harborough down by the starting line. He is riding too, I believe."

"I do not understand why the gentlemen ride too," ventured Lady Petley, who was breaking a silence that had lasted since they set off from the house. "They are not part of the race."

"It is permitted for owners to ride too," Drina explained.

"And preferable," added the Dowager, "to spectating with a group of hens who know nothing whatsoever about horse-racing.

"Is the filly in good heart?" she demanded a moment later.

"Simon's? She's been sweated and Simon is quite confident of her. Naturally all the horses from his stables are in good heart. Harborough's in particular."

At that moment Mr Fine sauntered up to their carriage and doffed his beaver. "Good day to you, ladies. Have you chosen the winner of this excellent field yet?"

Louisa giggled, and Lady Petley asked in a voice which seemed a little strained to Drina, "Which do you recommend, Mr Fine?"

He smiled urbanely, but his eyes were hard. Drina noticed this for the first time. "This is an opinion I prefer to keep to myself. However, I shall say that in racing, as in all things, the best man must always win."

"Do you wish your own colours were out there today?" Drina asked.

"Yes, indeed, Lady Arundale. But I am a patient man. One must often wait for victory."

Drina found conversing with Augustine Fine not at all easy and she turned instead to the old lady. "Mr Fine has bought a thoroughbred, Grandmama, to be trained at Simon's stables."

"There is no need to talk to me in that tone, Drina," she answered with some asperity. "I may be a trifle deaf and my eyes are certainly not as sharp as they once were, but I am not a babe in swaddling clothes." She raised her quizzing glass to study him the better. "What is this animal you have bought, Mr Fine?"

"A yearling, ma'am, and he is quite splendid. Lord Arundale is most impressed."

"Perhaps if you were to tell me its sire and dam I might be able to place it."

"The names elude me, Lady Arundale. Perhaps your grandson can enlighten you."

"No doubt he can. Call yourself a racing man, eh?"

"I do not style myself anything of the sort," he answered with aplomb.

"Tell me, Mr Fine, are you related to Sir Phineas Fine of Glendarrow, by any chance?"

"No, ma'am," he answered as urbanely as ever, and then, bowing briefly, he sauntered towards the starting line.

The Dowager allowed her glass to fall. "Can't pin that fellow down at all. He knows a little about everything, which in reality amounts to nothing about very much. There is something mighty fishy about that creature, if you ask me."

Drina smiled across at her cousin who was stifling a laugh behind her hand. As she did so Lady Petley gave a little gasp. When the others turned their attention upon her she said, "I cannot understand why we have to wait so long for the start of the race."

"Sometimes it takes an hour," Louisa pointed out.

"And more often than not a good deal longer," the Dowager added, with some small satisfaction. "Have you the flask of brandy, Drina?"

She obligingly produced the flask entrusted to her by Miss Rowlands and poured a measure for the Dowager, who took it in her gnarled hand. The old lady drank it down and handed it back to Drina just as Lady Petley got to her feet.

"I think I shall look at the horses at closer quarters. I would like to place a bet."

"Do take care with whom you place your bet, Lady Petley," Louisa warned. "I am forbidden because of the criminal element at courses."

As the attendant footman helped her down, Drina watched her anxiously. Was this just an excuse to be close to Simon for a while? she wondered. As Lady Petley hurried away Drina sought sight of him and spotted his tall figure near to Athena. He was conversing with Frogget who was dressed in the Earl's colours, a striking mixture of green, gold and orange. As the Earl moved away and mounted his own mare Drina drew a sigh of relief and said excitedly a moment later, "I believe they are about to begin." She peered around into the distance. "I wonder where Hélène could be. I cannot see her anywhere."

"I heard Petley had married a Frenchwoman," said the Dowager. "In Paris, wasn't it?"

"They met when the Allies entered Paris last year," Drina told her. "She was impoverished, but I believe she has rather illustrious ancestors. She is related to the Ducs de Cabouchard."

The old woman gave a dry throaty laugh. "Whoever that young lady is related to, it is *not* the Ducs de Cabouchard."

There was a moment's silence before Louisa said to Drina's further surprise, "*I* think she is absolutely charming."

The Dowager fixed the girl with her ferocious stare which caused Louisa's colour to heighten considerably. "And I did not say she was not."

An old gypsy woman approached the carriage and tried to persuade them to have their fortunes told, until the footmen turned her away, but a group of tumblers were allowed to perform and then suitably rewarded for their efforts.

Sir Francis came riding up to them, gazing in dismay at the empty seat in the carriage. "Where's Hélène?"

"Using her legs," answered the Dowager shortly, "and I wish I could do so too."

"Oh, they're off!" Louisa cried as Sir Francis continued to look around, presumably for sight of his wife, but the prospect of the race was enough to divert his mind.

"By jove, Athena's right out in front! No, it's Boynton's filly. Fine piece of horseflesh that. Wish she were mine."

"I do hope Candlemas wins," Louisa cried, jumping up and down with excitement. "Harborough's so anxious to win the Plate."

"We shall see. We shall see," answered the Dowager.

Drina herself caught the excitement too and sat tensely, her eyes glued to Frogget's bobbing figure. But at the back of her mind was that nagging worry about Lady Petley—and Simon.

"Dash it all!" exclaimed Sir Francis. "Boynton's in front and Frogget's falling behind. What on earth has got into him?" Drina gasped and clutched at her hands in alarm as a horse went down. "Hell's teeth, it's Boynton's filly that's gone down at the Ditch!" Sir Francis cried. "Nearly unseated Frogget, but he's still riding, Lady Arundale. Candlemas is well out in front now."

"I do hope Simon wins," the Dowager said with feeling. "He has wanted to win the Plate ever since I can recall."

"Athena's out ahead now. I'm sure it's Arundale's colours I can see," Louisa said breathlessly. "If Candlemas cannot win, then I hope Athena does."

"By jove! Miss Lythe is right. It is old Frogget. What a splendid show. Athena's out in front by a nose!"

A great cheer rose from the crowd and Drina could no longer contain her excitement and she jumped to her feet. "Arundale's filly has won, Grandmama!" she cried. "Oh, how wonderful that is!"

"In that case I shall have another brandy," she answered phlegmatically.

Drina sat down again, laughing. "It is cause for all of us to celebrate, Grandmama, and no doubt we shall do so tonight."

"This is *not* a celebration. It is necessary to keep me alive; it warms m'blood. That miserable creature, Rowlands, always tried to deprive me of it. Don't think I don't know why, even though she says it's because of the war and there isn't much brandy to be had, but there's no excuse now, is there? There is no war, and even so there was always brandy to be had if you knew where to get it."

Drina laughed again as she poured some brandy and handed it to her. "You know very well you are very fond of her. Oh, here comes Simon."

She experienced a familiar warmth the sight of him roused in her. After all these months of marriage she still felt shy in his presence, and now even more so. Since their guests had arrived, apart from those few moments last night, she had had little chance to be alone with him, much to her disappointment, and last night when she had retired very late the Earl had been engaged in a game of billiards with some of his friends. Drina had firmly decided to remain awake until he came up, but the events of the day had fatigued her and she fell fast asleep almost immediately she got into bed.

Without doubt, he was delighted with his long-awaited win and it did her heart good to see him so happy.

"That was closer than I would have cared for," he said, carrying the trophy triumphantly.

"Well, you won and that is what counts," his grandmother replied. "Well done, m'boy."

"That will make a fine addition to the trophy-room," Drina told him.

"In pride of place," he answered, handing it to her.

Sir Francis went to pump his hand and to slap his back. "The bookies will have to stump the blunt on this one, Simon. Guess what? There's a mill at Bury on Friday. Shropshire Sanderson is fighting Jed Nickleborough. Just heard about it. It will be well worth betting on, Simon."

"It sounds like a splendid idea. Shropshire Sanderson, eh? He's a real fighter. It will be a mill worth seeing."

"Ah, here comes Hélène," Drina reminded her husband.

Lady Petley was walking back towards them, her eyes downcast. "Where have you been, my love?" he asked. "Simon's filly won the Kelvington Plate."

Lady Petley managed a weak smile. "I am so glad, Lord Arundale."

Her husband glanced at her worriedly as he handed her into the carriage and the Earl gave the order for the horses to be reharnessed.

"It's time for the ladies to return to the house. Tomorrow's another day and you mustn't risk a chill, any of you."

None of them protested. It was much colder now and any other race could only be an anti-climax. It was rather a jubilant cavalcade which made its way back to Arundale Park that afternoon. The ladies drove back in their carriages and the gentlemen followed on horseback. Once they arrived and the drivers were riding away the carriages and the grooms taking away the horses, no one seemed anxious to go indoors despite the cold and the now failing light.

"If the weather holds, let us have our own race in the paddock on Thursday," one of the Earl's friends suggested. "No point in wasting good racing time just because the meeting's finished."

The Earl laughed. "Why not? It sounds like an excellent idea."

"I'll bet you a pony Simon'll win," Sir Francis challenged.

The ladies were making their way up the steps, everyone chattering at once, as was usual when females gather together, although on this occasion the men were no less exuberant. Two footmen were assisting the old Countess, who refused to be carried but paused to rest in the hall.

"It was a very exciting race," Drina said to Lady Petley, who seemed once more preoccupied with her own thoughts.

"Yes, indeed," she answered, coming out of her reverie with a visible start. "Lord Arundale had his heart set on winning, so I am glad he has had his wish."

Drina would have liked to have indulged in

further conversation with her friend, but the butler approached her, bearing a silver tray.

"My lady, several dispatches have arrived from London by special messenger whilst you were out."

As the amount of sealed packages on the tray was a large one and it was somewhat unusual Drina was surprised, but went on to say, "Then perhaps you had better distribute them, Carter."

"Very well, my lady."

The hall was filling up with people now. Miss Rowlands was fussing the Dowager, much to the old lady's annoyance, and the gentlemen were discussing the finer aspects of horse-racing, using graphic gestures to do so. The noise was almost deafening. Drina was still clutching the trophy which at last she pressed upon a footman, together with her muff.

Suddenly, as Drina began to unfasten her cloak, Sir Francis's voice could be heard clearly above all the others as he tore open his letter. "Good grief! This is terrible! Terrible!"

His wife ran up to him, placing a trembling hand on his arm. "Francis, what is wrong? What has happened?"

Sir Francis looked dazed. Silence had fallen on all the others, who had turned their attention upon Sir Francis, as he gazed around him without really seeing anyone at all.

"Napoleon's escaped from Elba and has

landed in France again. I must go to London immediately!"

His voice in the silence could not have broken more dramatic news, and for a moment there was no response, but when Lady Petley burst into a torrent of noisy tears pandemonium prevailed. All those who had also received dispatches tore them open. Sir Francis was in the Foreign Office, but many others were military men, recalled to their various regiments.

"This is dreadful news, Simon," Drina whispered to him as everyone began to talk at once, again.

He was looking very grim. "He will be stopped, of course, and perhaps he has been by this very minute." He glanced at her. "There will be much to do. We shall have to ensure all those who must leave immediately can do so with ease." He touched her arm as he began to move away. "I had best see that all the horses are ready for those who require them."

Lady Lythe chose at that moment to give way to the vapours and had to be led away by her daughter and future son-in-law, which relieved Drina of the responsibility as she knew there would be many other matters to which she would have to attend.

"My poor Hugo will be recalled too," Lady Lythe cried. "Oh, it is too bad just before

Louisa's wedding. Oh, that dreadful man. Why didn't they shoot him?"

She levelled a ferocious gaze on Lady Petley, who was being comforted by her husband. "How anyone could allow a Frenchwoman under his roof I shall never know. Treacherous! Not to be trusted, any of them!"

Louisa and Piers Harborough led her away as Hélène let out a cry of dismay and collapsed entirely in her husband's arms. Drina rushed forward as everyone ran here, there and everywhere, anxious to be away at the earliest possible moment. She helped Sir Francis lower his wife into a chair.

"It is only a swoon," Drina assured him as she brought a vinaigrette out of her reticule. "She will recover in a moment or two."

"That woman," he fumed. "I could strangle her. How could she possibly blame my poor Hélène? So innocent, so gentle. Why, if Boney was to see that old dragon he would turn tail and run!"

Drina suppressed a half-hysterical laugh as Lady Petley began to move once more. "My aunt, I regret, is not renowned for her tact or tolerance, Sir Francis."

"There, there, my love," he crooned as Lady Petley opened her eyes and looked dazedly all around her. "All will be well."

Recognition returned and she sat up slowly.

"Is it really true, Francis? That man is back in France?"

"You have nothing to fear, Hélène. You are in England now."

"Oh, Francis!" Her eyes filled with tears and she clutched at his hand. "This is dreadful news. What are we to do?"

Sir Francis looked uncomfortable. Drina replaced the vinaigrette in her reticule and straightened up. "I have been recalled immediately to London . . ."

"Don't leave me, Francis!" she begged, her eyes wide with fright. "I beg of you, do not leave me."

"It will only be for a little while, my love. Why, we shall have old Boney bottled up before you can blink an eye."

Lady Petley made a sound low in her throat and Sir Francis looked appealingly at Drina. "May I leave her in your care, Lady Arundale? There is no one else and I must go."

"You may rest assured, Sir Francis, Hélène will be well looked after in your absence."

He took his wife's hand in his and kissed it lovingly before hurrying to collect the valise his valet had hastily packed.

Hélène's eyes followed her husband longingly until Drina sat down beside her. "He will return before long, never you fear."

Lady Petley dabbed at her eyes with her handkerchief. "I am sure you are right. This has all been too much of a shock, though. Every-one was quite certain that monster was safely exiled. Now I am the enemy."

Drina was hard put not to laugh at such dramatic thoughts, but she said in a perfectly serious voice, "You do not have to mind Lady Lythe, you know."

"How can I mind what she says when I sympathise with her feelings? I am French, am I not? There is no changing that."

"Now, Hélène," she said in a matter-of-fact voice, beginning, in truth, to feel a little irri-tated now, "there is to be no more of the va-pours, do you understand?" Lady Petley gazed at her wide-eyed. "Time enough to indulge in hysterics when Boney lands on your doorstep."

"Do you really think that he will?" she asked in a frightened voice.

"Of course I don't!" Drina scoffed. "I am just attempting to make you see that everything is not quite so terrible, and besides you worry your husband so much, my dear. You must try not to, especially now when he will have a great deal of work thrust on him."

Lady Petley nodded as she dabbed at her eyes once more with the scrap of lace. "You are so full of good sense, Drina."

The other sighed. "So I am often told."

"And you are a good friend, and this worthless creature does not deserve your friend-ship."

Drina looked at her again, this time in alarm. "What . . . do you . . . mean, Hélène?"

Lady Petley shook her head and then buried it in her hands. "I just wish I were dead."

The Dowager Countess was still watching the hurry-scurry from her seat in the hall despite Miss Rowlands' constant urging to remove to a less draughty spot. With the door being constantly opened and shut, Miss Rowlands feared her mistress would contract some fatal chill, and proceeded to say so with irritating frequency.

"It would appear," she said to the man standing by her chair, "that those extravagant victory celebrations were a trifle premature this summer."

Mr Augustus Fine was also watching the departure of those recalled to their regiments. "I seem to recall saying something to that effect myself at the time, your ladyship," he answered, and had the old lady possessed a sharper eye she would not have missed the light of amusement which had lit up his face as he spoke.

NINE

ALTHOUGH so many of their guests had gone, a number of people still remained at Arundale Park, but the atmosphere was no longer jubilant or even mildly happy. The topic of conversation was Bonaparte, and conjecture about what he was likely to do now he was once more on French soil.

Lady Petley was a worry to Drina. She walked around now as white-faced as if she were a ghost.

"Simon," she whispered during the evening, "you will have to go and speak to Hélène. She is very despondent."

He looked at her in surprise as she carefully avoided meeting his eyes. "Why should I have any effect on her despondency?"

"Oh, I am sure your company will have a most beneficial effect on her," she replied, injecting a great deal of false gaiety into her voice.

"I should think it more likely your company will cheer her, now that you are able to devote more time to her. Lady Petley told me yesterday evening that she felt acutely the loss of intimacy between you of late."

Now Drina did look at him. "She told you this?"

"Expressly."

"You always seem so much in sympathy with her, though."

"I can't help it," he answered. "She's a fetching little thing and Francis adores her. Unenviable position too. There is no one else she can turn to except for us when Francis isn't here. Go along and cheer her up. She will be glad if you would do so."

"Even so, I know she would prefer a word from you, Simon."

He laughed. "I have never been very successful in dismissing the dismals from the female mind. Besides, your uncle, Harborough, Toby Denton and myself are about to engage in a rubber of whist."

So saying, he went to join them and Drina had no choice but to try and cajole her friend into a happier frame of mind, although she did think that men could be very selfish and un-feeling.

"Why don't you play for us a while?" she suggested to Lady Petley.

"I couldn't possibly."

"Are you certain my husband hasn't said something to put you out of countenance, Hélène? The other evening . . ."

Lady Petley looked at her in alarm. "No, no, Lord Arundale has always been so kind to me. I cannot imagine what put you in mind of such a thing."

"Then you must try hard to be brave, Hélène, for Sir Francis's sake if not for your own."

Lady Petley smiled. "I am a tiresome creature, am I not?"

"No, Hélène," Drina said softly, "we cannot always be bright and gay."

"But you are, and I know you cannot always be so happy."

"We all have our private sorrows," she answered soberly, "and I am not excepted. Now what do you wish to do? There is a long evening ahead of us and for once I am at your disposal."

"It has been a while, Drina. I was beginning to think perhaps I had offended you in some way."

Drina's heart was beating fast. "How could

that be, Hélène? Surely you are incapable of offending anyone."

Lady Petley was forced to look away, but Drina did not miss the paling of her cheeks which seemed to confirm all her fears and caused her heart to sink.

"Hutchings has set up the card tables, Hélène," she said a moment later, after swallowing the lump in her throat.

"Oh, yes," the Frenchwoman answered eagerly, "please do let us play bezique . . ."

The time came when Drina and her husband were alone at the foot of the staircase, having bid good night to the last of their guests to retire.

She turned and smiled at him shyly. "This houseparty will be talked of in times to come, Simon, but not, I fear, as we would wish."

"Trust Boney to take the thunder out of my best win yet." He gazed at her for a moment or two, which caused her blood to race. "You're looking pale again, Drina. The events of the last two days must have exhausted you. It will be relief, I dare say, when everyone has gone."

She was touched, as always, by his concern and was about to make some remark in reply when suddenly she frowned. "That is odd, Simon. I do not recall saying good night to Mr Fine."

"He is to leave in the morning and no doubt deemed it prudent to retire early. It is time we followed his good example."

She made no move to follow him and instead she continued to frown. "And I do not recall seeing Lady Petley of late, either."

"I am quite sure she is by now safely in her bed."

"No, I saw her walking towards the Conservatory some time ago, but I do not recall seeing her return."

"She is quite capable of walking back by herself. You mustn't be *too* anxious about her." She stared at him as he spoke, stiffening as always when he mentioned Lady Petley, listening for every nuance in his voice. Her face suddenly relaxed into a smile. "Today's events have really ruined your plans to hold a brilliant party, haven't they, Drina?"

"Is that what you think I really wanted?" she asked in a bleak voice.

"I think you intend, in time to come, to go down in the history books as the most brilliant hostess of 1815."

She turned away from him as he teased her. Haughtily she answered, "You have a strange opinion of me when our country is poised on the edge of war again."

"I also think that fatigue makes you tetchy . . ."

He was talking to her in that indulgent way which made her feel as though she were no

more than a child, and she hated it. She wanted
him to look on her as a woman, a woman with
so much love in her heart for him, but it
seemed, even now, this was impossible. She was
his wife and as such useful to provide him with
a much-wanted heir. Love could be obtained
elsewhere.

He was going up the stairs. Most of the
candles had already been snuffed by the servants
and the house was growing dim.

"I must make certain Hélène is not still
downstairs," she murmured, and hurried away
from him before he could protest or suggest he
send a footman. Truth to tell, Drina was less
than anxious to join him in their rooms. There
was so large a difference between love and duty.
She felt one and he the other, and there was no
way of reconciling the two.

There were no lights in the Conservatory,
and having reached it Drina realised that
Hélène could not possibly be there. With the
aid of the moonlight which was streaming in
through each of the many windows she could
see the outline of the seats and the tall stone
pillars which soared up to support a glass dome.
Just as she was about to go back out of the
Conservatory she hesitated, having heard a
noise. It was no more than a whisper there in
the darkness, and then, listening carefully, she
realised it was the sound of sobbing she had
heard.

Hélène! Drina moved forward slowly, some instinct deep within her telling her to tread warily. Why was Hélène crying there in the dark?

"Stop this foolishness!" came a harsh voice which made Drina freeze on the spot.

She was very near to them, she realised, hidden by a pillar. Something told her not to reveal herself, that there was a furtiveness about their presence at this time of the night.

"I will tolerate no more of it, Hélène. You will continue to do as you are told or face the consequences."

"Oh, I cannot, Andre. Please have mercy on me. These people are my friends and I cannot betray them. They have been so kind to me."

"Kind," the man sneered. "They are aristocrats, so bloated with their own importance they cannot see the misery of others. Do you think they will be so *kind* to you if they knew just who and what you are?"

Drina pressed her knuckle into her mouth to suppress a cry. Andre! It was Mr Fine she had called Andre. Thoughts whirled round in her head, incoherent and without form, but she didn't doubt she had stumbled on to something strange.

"I can do no more without raising Francis's suspicions. Already my friends look at me strangely."

"Then you must learn to control yourself better. Listen to me, you useless woman," he said with such ferocity Drina was tempted to reveal herself in order to demand a stop to this bullying. "You will continue to report to me on every scrap of information you can glean. Now, more than ever, the Emperor needs your information."

"But now England will be at war again and I cannot do it, Andre. Not now. You must understand."

The man laughed, but it was not a pleasant sound. "Stupid woman. Do you not realise it is directly due to the information you have supplied that the Emperor has chosen this time to leave Elba?"

"Oh, no!"

Hélène began to cry again, but this time Drina was not moved. All was now clear to her and she was in an agony of indecision. She was torn between the desire to fetch help and curiosity to learn more. She decided to remain, for to move now would be to reveal herself, and she knew that could prove to be very dangerous.

To think, she and the Earl had been harbouring a French spy in their home! And Hélène? How on earth had she been inveigled into his devilish schemes? Drina wondered.

"That just is not possible," Hélène sobbed.

"Why?" The question came as sharp as a whip. "Could that be because you have been withholding some information from me after all?" he asked in a cold voice.

"No! But I thought . . ."

"You thought because the Emperor was safe in exile and Europe at peace Andre Furneaux was amusing himself with a few games, indulging his old tricks quite harmlessly. You underestimate me, my dear. You have been useful to me, but I have many spies working for me all over England."

Drina, listening and hardly daring to breathe, wondered why this man's evil had not been evident to them before.

"I will . . . not help you any . . . more," gasped Lady Petley.

"Yes you will, my dear." His voice was almost kind, but the menace in him was still unmistakable. "Because if you do not, I shall introduce myself to Sir Francis. 'Good day to you, sir,' I shall say. 'Allow me to introduce myself; Andre Furneaux, and this is my charming wife, Hélène Furneaux.' "

Drina felt quite ill. So that was the answer, the reason Hélène was so much in his power. She was horrified, gripping hold of the pillar with clammy hands.

Lady Petley moaned. "But when I married Francis I thought you were dead. I had been told you were dead."

The man chuckled evilly. "The poor, grieving widow. Who, do you think, will believe that?"

"If you tell him you will reveal yourself for what you are. You will go to prison as a spy, and I am not so foolish as to believe you would bring such a fate upon yourself."

"Oh, my dear," he said in a pitying voice, "not prison. We shall both go to the gibbet unless, of course, my helpers in this country contrive to rescue me, which is very possible. Naturally, they will not be able to save us both, I fear. You will hang for treason, despised by all those good friends of yours."

After waiting a moment for the implication of his words to sink into her mind, he continued in a more brisk tone, "Tomorrow you are to make some excuse to the Countess and return to London—to be near your husband, as any devoted wife would be. I shall expect to hear from you frequently. It is more imperative than ever now for you to give me any piece of information you can glean from your . . . husband and his friends. He is besotted by you; he will tell you everything, if only you will ask, and I shall be content with nothing less than everything."

"Have pity on me," she moaned, but he did not hear. He was walking quickly away from her. As his footsteps receded Drina let out a long breath which she had been holding for some time and moved from behind the pillar.

Hélène was sitting on the bench, staring into the darkness. She had stopped sobbing, much to Drina's relief. She felt she could not cope with another attack of the vapours that day.

"Hélène," she said, keeping her voice to a whisper.

The Frenchwoman's head snapped round and a look of horror crossed her face. "Drina, what are you doing here? I thought everyone was in bed."

Her eyes were wide with fright as she looked beyond Drina into the darkness. "It is quite all right, Hélène. He has gone."

She gasped. "You saw him?"

Drina sank down next to her on the bench. "And I heard everything—at least enough to understand."

"What will you do?" she asked in a frightened voice.

"That is something we must decide between us, Hélène. First you must tell me everything. I must know the truth."

Hélène wrung her hands together. "I cannot. You heard him. He is ruthless and I am afraid of what he will do."

"You cannot possibly fight him on your own, but he must be brought to book, and soon. He is a spy, a danger to England. . . ."

"No one can do anything to stop him. I know him. He is always triumphant and I am a wretched creature. Everyone will despise me."

Drina put one hand over hers. "No one will despise you unless you give in to him still. You do have friends here, Hélène, whatever that man says. Everyone will want to help you."

"There is no help for me now. I am doomed."

"Don't give in to such sentiments. Is it true he is your husband?"

"Yes," she answered, her voice almost breaking, "but I vow I did not know he was still alive when I married Francis. Oh, Francis! I cannot bear to think of him."

"You have been passing information to this French spy, haven't you?"

"I tried to ensure I told him nothing of very great importance. Indeed, it would have been difficult to do any other, for Francis tells me so little about his work."

"And I am convinced, my dear, whatever you did it was under duress."

"Of course it was! Why else would I betray him! I love him so much, Drina." She turned her large, tear-filled eyes on her friend. "You could not imagine how it is with me. To live in such despair and then to find a man as wonderful as Francis, to live in this way after the depths I am used to . . ."

Drina smiled grimly in the darkness. "Oh, yes, Hélène, I can so easily imagine it."

"When I married Andre he seemed such a kind and decent man, but I soon discovered he was a devil. He is one of Bonaparte's spy-masters, which I did not know when I married him. My life with him was miserable. He was always so cruel, but as you have seen for yourself he can so easily deceive people into believing him good and kind. I used to dread him coming home. I would have run away from him so many times, only there was nowhere for me to go, and I knew as a point of honour he would find me and bring me back.

"And then came the abdication. I heard that Andre had been killed, and although I had little money and no home any more I rejoiced at my freedom from his tyranny. But it was hard. I was forced to sleep in an abandoned house for a while, but when the Allies came to celebrate all deserted houses were put into use, so I was forced to sleep outdoors, gaining what shelter I could. I dreaded the coming winter. I tried to find work—any work, so long as it paid me enough to buy a little food and some warm clothing, but there was no work to be had and soon I had no money at all. I was hungry until I met a Prussian officer who gave me a meal. It was not until after I had eaten that I realised why he had been so generous to me." She buried her face in her hands. "I cannot tell you."

Drina gazed at her compassionately, her heart full of pain. "It's all right, Hélène. I do understand."

"After a struggle I managed to run away from him. I was in such despair, Drina. I only wanted to die and I was determined to kill myself, and that was when Francis found me.

"You cannot imagine how kind he was. He took me to a grand lady who cared for me for days while I was so ill with the fever. She gave me food and clothes, and a kindness I had not known since I was a child. And I could scarce believe my luck when Francis said he loved me and wanted me for his wife. I adored him."

Drina felt the tears welling up in her own eyes and trickle on to her cheeks.

"It was heaven for a while. Such happiness could not last, and it didn't. One day Andre presented himself to me. I was so distraught. You see, he knew very well I was not of aristocratic birth. My father was a shoemaker and my mother an abigail, and Andre threatened to reveal all this as well as his own identity to Francis if I did not help him. I could not bear Francis to know, to have to go back perhaps to Andre again."

"Francis would not have allowed that to happen."

"Perhaps not, but I was too distraught even to think very clearly at that time. I agreed to help Andre because I did not think it mattered when Bonaparte was in exile and his army disbanded. I thought I could humour and indulge Andre with a little information now and again.

I vow I never revealed anything that could be of use to the French."

"I think it likely Mr Fine exaggerates so as to keep you under his control. Any information you give from now on could be of much greater use to him."

"He will learn nothing now, Drina." She glanced at her friend curiously. "You do not shrink from me."

"I have no cause to, my dear. All will be well, you will see."

"Oh, I pray that you are right. Do you wonder I didn't want to come here this week when I discovered he was to be here also? I felt by not denouncing him it was my fault that he had fooled his way into the homes of my friends. What am I to do? I cannot continue with this pretence, Drina, and yet if I confess. . . ." She gripped Drina's arm. "Please tell me what I must do."

"I don't know," she admitted. "You must give me time to consider the best course to take, Hélène." She turned to look at her. "There is just one thing I must ask . . ."

"Anything. You know everything now. I have no secrets from you any more."

"You say you are in love with Sir Francis."

She looked away quickly as Lady Petley said, "Do you doubt it? There has never been any other man in my life whom I have loved."

Drina drew a sigh. She believed Hélène implicitly, and so there must be some other explanation for Simon's presence in the corridor that night, but it was of so little importance now. Hélène truly expected her to find a solution to the horrific dilemma, but she could envisage none.

"Hélène," she said after a moment, "nothing more can be decided tonight. Go to bed and try to rest. I shall think on it in the meanwhile."

"You will not tell anyone, will you?"

"Simon will have to know, but perhaps not tonight," she answered gently. "Go along now and try not to tease yourself. There is a solution if only we can find it, and you are not alone."

Lady Petley hugged her friend close to her. "You will not fail me, I know it. Only, Francis must not know. That is all I ask."

All! It was impossible for Sir Francis to remain in ignorance, but Drina could not tell her so now.

"You are not going to remain here by yourself, are you?" asked Lady Petley as she stood up to go.

"For a few minutes, so that I can think. I shall be along presently." She looked up at her. "Good night, Hélène, and do not worry."

As she went out of the Conservatory Drina drew another sigh. How to bring a spy to book and at the same time protect Hélène. It was impossible. Drina knew she would have to inform someone, but the problem of not implicating Hélène was insurmountable. Whichever way Drina considered the matter Hélène was going to be in serious trouble, if not from the ruthless Frenchman or the British Government, then with Sir Francis, who believed in her implicitly.

Suddenly she thought she heard a noise near the entrance to the Conservatory and her heart began to race. She listened for a few moments and when she heard nothing more she relaxed again, but she realised she had been sitting there for quite some time and if she was not to rouse the Earl's suspicions she must go to him now. On learning there was no relationship between Hélène and her husband a great burden had been lifted from her mind, only to be replaced by one equally as heavy.

She got to her feet. Simon! Of course. He *could* help. His godfather was Lord Castlereagh himself.

"Simon can go directly to Lord Castlereagh and get immunity for Hélène," she said aloud as she hurried from the Conservatory.

"I am afraid I cannot allow that, Lady Arundale," came a voice from the darkness.

Drina gasped in alarm, but before she could cry out loud a hand was clamped over her mouth and she was being gripped tightly from behind.

"Take her to my room, Bonnier, until we decide what to do with her."

The footmen had now retired and the hall

through which she was being bundled by Andre Furneaux's manservant was deserted and in darkness. Foolish to believe so ruthless a man would be alone. She hoped Simon would come to find her, but she doubted that he would. The last place anyone would look for her would be in Mr Fine's room, and by the time she was missed it could be too late anyway.

Bonnier threw her unceremoniously on to the bed and as she struggled to sit up she found herself looking into the smiling face of the man she had known as Augustus Fine, aspiring racehorse owner. How he must have been laughing at them all these months as he patiently insinuated his way into the topmost echelon of British Society. Still he looked debonair and charming, only he was holding a pistol level with her face.

"Now, my dear, do be sensible, won't you? If you scream I shall shoot the first man who comes to your aid and it might well be Lord Arundale."

"How dare you threaten me and treat me so in my own house!"

"It was never planned to do so, Lady Arundale, believe me. Blame yourself, my dear, for a curiosity which involved you in matters which do not concern you in the slightest."

"The plight of a friend needs must concern me."

"Then that is your misfortune."

"I demand that you let me go."

"I am afraid I cannot."

"I shall be missed. My husband . . ."

"But the time he realises you are missing and instigates a search. . . . Well, it is fortunate for us he owns such a grand house. So many rooms. And the outbuildings and grounds. Oh, I fancy we shall be long gone by then, Lady Arundale, and no one will know where, even if I am suspected rather than thought to have made an early start to the journey already announced."

"Hélène will tell."

He chuckled softly. "You think so? Recall she will hang if she implicates herself. Ah, at last I have an idea."

"What are you going to do to me?" she asked, afraid now.

"Well, now, I shall have to think about that a little longer, my dear. My foolish wife, in telling you all, has caused me a great deal of trouble. Oh, yes, I knew you were behind that pillar, but unfortunately not soon enough. Pity, this is a complication I would rather have avoided. I shall have to tread very warily if I am not to reveal myself."

"You dare not harm me."

"I shall not wish to, unless you behave foolishly. I merely wish to turn this unfortunate situation into one advantageous to me."

"My husband will kill you when he catches you," she gasped, near to tears but too proud to show it.

"*If* he catches me."

He turned away, but there was no advantage to that. Bonnier, now she could see him at close quarters, looked a rough individual and he was stationed by the door.

"Kill her, monsieur," he suggested, and there was an eager light in his eyes as he spoke.

"Then nothing will stop my wife from telling all. I have a scheme which will ensure her silence." He looked at Drina again and she was still feeling bruised and shaken after such a rough manhandling.

"You, I think, my dear, are not so easily influenced as Madame Furneaux."

"To me she is, and always will be, Lady Petley."

He turned on his heel. "I shall write a note to 'Lady Petley'," he announced, and sitting down at the desk he proceeded to do so whilst Bonnier continued to watch Drina. For a few minutes nothing could be heard save the scratching of his pen on the parchment, and then he folded it and inserted the page into an envelope.

"Push this beneath Lady Petley's door, Bonnier, and then have the carriage made ready. Lady Arundale is going to make a little journey."

"I have no intention of leaving my home!"

"I agree that you have a choice. You can leave here alive, my dear, or remain here dead."

Drina gasped again and the manservant laughed. She guessed that this man would take great pleasure in killing her, and for all his urbane manner Monsieur Furneaux was a dangerous adversary. It was only at that moment that she started to be really afraid, for up until then she had told herself this man would not dare to harm her under the roof of Arundale Park.

When Bonnier had gone he addressed her once more. "I have some important information which has been gathered by my spies all over England. A boat is waiting to transport it to France, and we shall be on it also. I believe it is time for me to return to the direct service of my Emperor, although I had not yet planned to do so. Unfortunately, it seems that my useful life here is over."

"You cannot take me to France!"

He merely laughed before he added, "I have informed my wife that if she speaks about me once you are discovered missing, and if any attempt at pursuit is made, you will be put overboard halfway across the Channel. I vow she will remain silent. Her own life is at stake too."

Drina's head drooped. "I am of no use to you, so you will kill me whatever Hélène may do."

He made no answer. He merely took a leather pouch from a drawer in the dresser and put it into his pocket. "This must be delivered to the Emperor himself. It is most important."

"What do you intend to do with me?" she demanded to know.

He gazed at her. "You have spoiled a great many of my plans. There was still a great deal of work for me to do here and your curiosity has caused me a mite of trouble, which is a pity because I admire you, Lady Arundale, and have done so for some time."

He turned away from her and she sank back on the point of exhaustion on the bed. Simon, she thought. Oh, Simon, I do love you, and you will not grieve long for me.

All too soon Bonnier returned. "The carriage is ready, and the hooves of the horses are muffled."

"The note has been delivered?"

"*Certainement, monsieur*. But we must leave immediately if we are to reach the coast before daybreak."

Andre Furneaux went to the press and brought out a box coat which he handed to Drina. "We should hate for you to *freeze* to death, my lady," he said mockingly. "Your gown is hardly made for warmth."

In her fine gauze gown Drina felt naked beneath his gaze and was glad enough to put on the man's box coat which enveloped her completely, but she wasn't sure that freezing to death was not more preferable to drowning. At the thought of this very real danger she began to tremble. The Earl was not so far away, in the next corridor, but she dare not call out.

Before he opened the door Andre Furneaux reminded her. "Remember, Lady Arundale, I shall kill the first man who comes to your aid."

Drina didn't doubt it. All was quiet as the man peered up and down the corridor, and then when he nodded Bonnier took her arm roughly and pulled her to her feet. He did not notice the monogrammed handkerchief which she left on the bed, although Drina wasn't sure what she hoped to achieve by so doing. Neither did she know whether she was relieved or disappointed when they encountered no one on their journey downstairs.

The night was bitingly cold and she shuddered as the force of the wind hit her. The water would be cold too but she would not let her mind dwell on that thought. Bonnier had brought out a carriage, one that was small and neat and suited the man who owned it. As Bonnier pushed her inside she glanced upwards in one last despairing gesture. A light was still burning in the Earl's dressing-room and she didn't doubt he would be discussing the day's events with his valet, unaware and perhaps even uncaring about his wife. A familiar lump rose in her throat as she squeezed herself into the far corner of the carriage as far away from Andre Furneaux as she could contrive.

As soon as Andre Furneaux was seated the carriage set off. "I apologise that there is no brick to warm my lady's feet and no fur rug to warm my lady's knees."

"Why do you hate us so, Monsieur Furneaux?"

"I do not hate you, my lady, for no one could hate someone so fair, but I do despise your way of life."

Drina stared at him with interest now. "You cannot change anything. What can you possibly gain by this?"

"Power, my dear. An important post here in England has been promised to me by the Emperor himself." Drina shuddered at the very thought. "He is very satisfied with my efforts here in England. I have served him well."

"You cannot possibly beat the British. Bonaparte tried for most of my life and failed. He cannot succeed now."

His eyes flashed with anger and Drina was immediately reminded that this was not the mild-mannered Mr Augustus Fine, but a dangerous spy, and once again she was afraid. They were passing through the gates of Arundale Park and Andre Furneaux relaxed visibly.

"There is little chance of pursuit now if no one heard us leave, so you may as well doze, my dear. We have a substantial ride before us."

The horses were charging forward into the night; Drina felt its darkness envelop her. She thought she had never felt more desolate. She would never see Simon again.

TEN

THE carriage jerked to a halt and Drina woke with a start, thankful to be awake at last, for she had endured a frightening dream. As she gazed around her she cried out, realising that it had not been a dream after all. It was all true. She was a prisoner of this fiend and at his mercy.

It was light now and she realised they had been travelling through the night. Her limbs were so cramped and cold she could scarcely move them and when she did it was a painful experience.

"Journey's end, my dear," Andre Furneaux told her, "or almost." He looked fresh and alert, but she doubted that he had slept at all.

As Bonnier opened the carriage door and let

down the steps Andre Furneaux climbed down and gave her his hand. "No," she said firmly. "I shall not move from this carriage."

The Frenchman smiled. "Bonnier! I believe the Countess needs persuading to alight."

The big man moved as if to grasp her and it was then that Drina moved, scorning a helping hand and almost stumbling to the ground. Andre Fureaux steadied her, and although she hated the touch of either of these men she certainly preferred that of Andre Furneaux to his manservant.

"Bonnier, conceal the carriage," Furneaux told him as he took Drina's arm to lead her to a cottage which appeared to be on the outskirts of a village. Overhead gulls wheeled in the early morning sun, so she guessed the sea was not far away. As she was hurried towards the cottage she looked around for a source of assistance, but there was no one. The village itself was too far away to attempt even a shout.

She was propelled roughly into the only downstairs room the cottage possessed. A woman was bending over a cauldron suspended above the fire, and she straightened up quickly as they entered, wiping her hands on her apron and bobbing a curtsey. Her eyes opened wide at the sight of Drina in Andre Furneaux's coat, the diamond necklace still about her neck and visible beneath the collar.

"Have we missed the tide?" he demanded.

There was no attempt at charm with this woman.

"Aye, sir, three hours ago the boats went out."

"Ah, we could have put to sea with the fishing boats and that way we would not have aroused suspicion. We shall have to go at nightfall instead. An unfortunate delay, but unavoidable. Bring us victuals, woman, and be quick about it."

The woman continued to watch as Drina was propelled forward towards some rickety steps. She struggled to mount them, hampered by the box coat and her ankle-length gown. The steps led to an attic with a sloping roof and a small window with a view of the sea. The only furniture was a truckle bed, a rickety table and a chair. Drina was pushed roughly towards the bed and she fell on it, gasping for breath. After a moment or two, as she began to recover herself a little, she began to chafe her frozen hands, glad that the attic was at least warmed by the fire in the hearth downstairs.

"Why can't you just leave me here when you go?" she asked in a broken voice.

He went to gaze out of the window. "This house is valuable to our agents who might wish to cross to France. We have used it since before Trafalgar and we shall want to use it again." He looked at her. "You may as well settle down to wait. We shall be here for some hours."

Time for rescue, she thought, but it did not cheer her. Time, perhaps, but the possibility was as remote as ever.

A sound on the steps made Drina stiffen, but it was only the woman, who was carrying a tray on which stood two bowls of something which steamed.

"Not quite up to the standards of Arundale Park," the man commented as the woman put the tray on the table.

She stared at Drina once more, at the splendour of her gown which was visible now she had allowed the coat to fall open a little.

Andre Furneaux did not miss her curiosity either. "You have a very important guest here today, madam."

The woman turned her frightened eyes on him. "Will there be trouble?"

"Not for you, good lady, if you obey my orders. We shall be gone at nightfall and there will be nought to say the Countess of Arundale was ever here."

She hurried down the stairs and he brought Drina a bowl of the revolting-looking concoction, and the coarse bread which was cut into unappetising chunks. A fish gruel, she thought, looking into the bowl with distaste. But it was hot and nourishing, and she was cold and hungry. In a few moments it was gone and she felt much better although no less afraid.

She looked at this man curiously as he relished the last drop of the gruel. "When we were children our nanny frightened us with tales of Bonaparte. She said that if we were naughty he would come and eat us."

Andre Furneaux put down his bowl and laughed. "The only thing that frightened me as a child was my empty stomach. Bonaparte is a great man. One day he will rule the entire world."

Drina looked away quickly, for she dare not risk his wrath by contradicting him. A moment later there came the sound of a door closing downstairs and she knew a momentary hope until her captor said, "Bonnier must be back."

He went across to the steps and paused. "Do not think to try and escape, Lady Arundale. Bonnier and I will be just downstairs."

As he clattered down the steps Drina buried her head in her hands, unable to fight back her tears any longer. She was so afraid. There could be no compromise with these people.

At the sound of someone entering the room she looked up, gasping back her tears. It was the fisherman's wife, come to take back the tray. As on the previous occasion, she stared at Drina with a great deal of curiosity and Drina realised that this woman might never have seen so grand a dress or such magnificent jewellery before.

She put her hand out to the woman, who immediately snatched hers away. "Please, you must help me," she pleaded, her voice a whisper.

The woman shook her head in mute terror and would have hurried away if Drina had not said, putting her hand to her throat, "You like these, don't you? They're real diamonds. A fortune in diamonds; enough to set you up in style. A house, a carriage, all the clothes you could wish for, and they can be yours if you help me escape from here."

She shook her head again. "You must not ask. 'Tis impossible. What good would jewels be to me? He'd cut my throat."

As she hurried downstairs Drina sank back on to the truckle bed, despair and exhaustion overcoming her at last, and even when her captor returned she did not stir.

He came across the room and stood gazing down on her. "You have my admiration, Lady Arundale, for not making matters more difficult for yourself."

"If I thought there was a chance at all of escaping from this place I would take it," she told him in a tired voice.

"But wisely you have resisted all temptation to try. It would be most inadvisable." There was a moment's pause before he went on, "You may not be aware of this, Lady Arundale, but I have admired you for many months past." He laughed deprecatingly. "Naturally, to show you my admiration would have been most improper, but that hardly applies now, does it? There can be no social barriers here where there is no one to see us."

She sat up now and drew the coat about her. "I would be obliged if you would leave me alone. I have no taste for company."

He chuckled. "My wife would have been having the vapours long ago had she been in your situation."

"I may surprise you yet."

He came to sit beside her on the truckle bed, a move which alarmed her anew. She moved as far away as she could, pressing herself against the wall, although in such a confined space it was impossible to be out of reach.

"We have many hours ahead of us," he said in a soft voice which made her cringe. "It is possible by the time we leave I may have decided to take you all the way to France with me. . . . It is up to you to persuade me of the wisdom of that course."

Drina shuddered as he stared at her with those hard little eyes. He put one hand out to touch her and she flinched away from him.

"Come now, my dear, surely you realise you have a way of saving yourself."

She shuddered yet again. "I would prefer to die."

All bonhomie was gone from his manner now as his cheeks flooded with colour, but he still smiled which terrified her all the more. "You have no choice! You are my prisoner and you will do as I say. I am not one of the servants at Arundale Park to be dismissed when it pleases you."

She pressed herself further against the wall, her eyes wide with fear as his face twisted into a grimace of rage and he lurched towards her. She kicked out at him but missed and he threw her down on to the bed. She resisted him by trying to claw at his face, but he was far too powerful for her to succeed in resisting him for long, and he managed to press his lips against hers. She kept on pummelling his back with her fists and tried to turn her face away, but he caught her hands easily and, pinning them down, he continued to press feverish kisses against her face.

"For pity's sake, kill me now," she gasped.

"Furneaux!"

The man stumbled to his feet on hearing the unfamiliar voice call his name, relieving Drina of his weight and obnoxious presence. Furneaux whirled round, freezing on the spot and Drina cried out with fear and joy at the sight of the Earl standing in the doorway. He had his pistols levelled at the Frenchman and his eyes which were heavy with fatigue were glittering with hatred.

"I should kill you now, and if you move one muscle I promise that I will. Drina, come over here by me."

She needed no further urging. Scrambling to her feet, she rushed across the room to his side. "Oh, Simon, I'm so glad you're here. Did you deal with Bonnier?"

"Bonnier?" He still kept his eyes firmly on the Frenchman, whose face took on a crafty look.

"The manservant," Drina said impatiently. "He was on guard downstairs."

"There was no one downstairs. Go, Drina," he said, and there was no mistaking the urgency in his voice. "The militia is on its way. It will be arriving presently and then we can be sure Monsieur Furneaux receives his dues, but in the meantime there is no way of knowing how many rats are in this particular pack."

Even as he spoke there came a noise on the steps and Drina saw Bonnier. She cried out a warning, but it was too late. As the Earl turned to deal with him, Bonnier had hit him a glancing blow on the side of his head. The pistols clattered to the floor and the Earl slumped forward into unconsciousness before his wife's horrified eyes. She sank down beside him as blood began to ooze out of a wound on his temple.

"Simon! My love, speak to me."

The Frenchman rushed forward and stared down at the Earl as Drina lamented over the inert form of her husband. She looked up at her captor, tears sparkling in her eyes.

"You must help him. I'll do anything you ask of me if only you will help him."

"There is no time. You heard him say the militia is on its way. Bonnier, where *were* you?"

"Round the back of the cottage, monsieur. Only went for a minute, as a necessity."

Andre Furneaux made a sound of annoyance. "There has been one problem on top of another. First Hélène, then you, Countess, and now this ... How did he find us?"

"Told you, monsieur, we should have killed her. We'd never have had this problem if we had."

"Yes, yes, I know. Well, it's too late now. Perhaps my lady will be our means of getting out of here after all. Fetch the horses, Bonnier. We must not delay a moment longer."

The manservant rushed to do his master's bidding and as he did so Drina took the Earl's head in her lap, cradling it and trying to stop the bleeding. Andre Furneaux began to pace the tiny room, cursing in French at this hitch to his plans. Drina glanced at him fearfully; a wild animal became dangerous when cornered.

Suddenly her tears began to flow again, although she fought them back. Somehow he had found her and they were so nearly free. Now she didn't know whether he was dead or alive.

There came the sound of a shot downstairs,

followed immediately by a cry, which made Drina start. The Frenchman grew pale.

"Bonnier," he shouted, but there was no reply. "Bonnier!"

He drew his own pistol and began to pull Drina to her feet. Resisting him, she cried, "Leave me here! Let me be with him, I beg of you."

The man was so beside himself he did not even hear her plea. Holding her tightly, he began to pull her towards the stairs. Just then something inside Drina snapped and she began to pummel him with her fists.

"Leave me alone, you fiend! Don't dare to touch me again. You've killed him. You've killed him and I hate you! Murderer! Murderer!"

The Frenchman slapped her so hard across the face that she fell back and banged her head against the wall, dazing her for a moment.

"If you do not do as you are told, madam, I shall put a shot through his brain and make quite sure he is dead."

He took hold of her again and half dragged, half pushed her down the stairs. She landed on her knees on the floor below, tears blinding her eyes and sobs racking her body. Andre Furneaux stooped to raise her to her feet and as he did so an authoritative voice ordered, "Leave her, Andre."

Both he and Drina looked up to see Hélène

Petley standing in the doorway; the pistol in her hand was pointed at the Frenchman. Both Drina and her captor stared in astonishment. She was as immaculately dressed and coiffeured as if she were about to go to a ball, but incongruously she was holding that deadly weapon in her bejewelled hands.

"Don't be a fool, Hélène," he said contemptuously after recovering from his surprise. "Let us pass."

Drina had never seen Hélène look so calm or so much in possession of herself. "I allowed you to terrorise my own life, but did you really believe I would allow you to hurt *her*?"

His eyes narrowed craftily again. "You forget, Hélène, what you have to lose."

Lady Petley threw back her head proudly. "I have nothing to lose, except fear. Francis knows everything—my background, and whatever I have done under duress he has understood and forgiven."

"He may be besotted enough to do so, but the same will not apply to his country."

"He says any information I may have passed on to you is of no importance at all to the enemy, but what I have told him about this place is, so, you see, Andre, I am more likely to be considered a heroine when this is over. Francis will be here at any moment with the soldiers, and when you are hanged I shall ensure I am there to enjoy the spectacle."

"A detachment of troops cannot move so fast, so I have time to escape. You will not stop me."

He started forward and Hélène raised the pistol in line with his heart again. "I stopped Bonnier."

Furneaux hesitated for a moment, still unsure about her. A calculating look came into his eyes again. He still had hold of Drina's arm and suddenly he pulled her forward in an attempt to shield himself, and it was then that Hélène pulled the trigger. Both watched in horror as the man crumpled and fell to the floor, blood gushing from a wound in his chest, and then Hélène and Drina were holding on to each other, laughing and crying all at once.

"Is it true, Hélène? Does Francis know all?"

She nodded breathlessly. "'He does not care a jot about the past. He always suspected I was not an aristocrat anyway."

"I'm so glad."

Just then there came the sound of horses at the gallop and shouting, and a moment later the tiny cottage was filled with scarlet uniforms. Sir Francis came rushing into the cottage, his pistol at the ready. He stopped in the doorway, taking in the scene before him, and his face paled at the sight of his wife and the dead spy on the floor.

"Hélène!" She went to him immediately. "I thought you were to remain at Arundale Park."

"I could not allow Lord Arundale to come alone, Francis. It was all my fault . . ."

"Are you unhurt, Lady Arundale?" he asked, looking to her anxiously.

"Yes. Hélène shot Furneaux to save me. She was so brave." Her face suddenly crumpled and her eyes filled with tears. "But Simon . . ."

She rushed up the stairs with her friends in close pursuit, only to find the Earl sitting up, holding his head and gazing around him dazedly.

"Oh, Simon!" she cried, throwing her arms around him. "You are safe. Thank God!"

He stared at her. "What has happened?"

Sir Francis bent to examine the wound on which the blood was already congealing. "Nothing serious there, old boy. Hélène, fetch some water."

"What is Lady Petley doing here? We left her at Arundale Park, didn't we?"

"Hush," Drina urged, stroking his face lovingly. "Rest a while and we shall tell you all later."

"Furneaux?"

"Dead," she answered breathlessly. "And Bonnier too."

As Sir Francis helped him to his feet the Earl gripped hold of Drina. "Did that swine hurt you, Drina?"

She shook her head, smiling through her tears. "I am quite all right. Quite all right."

He did not relinquish his hold on her. "But your gown is all covered with blood."

She looked down to see that this was true. "It's your blood, Simon," she answered in dismay. "Your head was in my lap for a while."

He let out a long breath. "Thank God it wasn't yours."

Just as he sank down on the bed Lady Petley came scrambling back up the stairs with a bowl out of which water was splashing all about. The Earl looked alarmingly pale and they all watched him anxiously as he sank back on to the one dirty pillow.

Watching Drina gently bathe the wound, Sir Francis said, "I think, Hélène, you and I had better go downstairs and leave Simon to rest. He looks all knocked up."

"You can take credit for that too, Francis," his friend said in as severe a tone as he could manage.

Drina paused to look at them both curiously. "Sir Francis?"

Both he and his wife looked shamefaced and it was Hélène who went on to explain, "When Francis arrived at Arundale Park he found me being consoled by Lord Arundale, and I am afraid he acted a little . . . hastily."

The Earl put his hand to the other side of his head as Drina began to laugh.

"Thought Simon had been deceiving me all

this time," Sir Francis muttered, and then, "Come along, Hélène. Let's go downstairs."

"Before we go I must tell you that the soldiers have arrested the fisherman's wife as she ran away from here and they will be waiting for her husband when he returns."

"So all is finished here," Sir Francis answered with satisfaction, gazing down into his wife's face. "That is good."

"There are some important papers in Furneaux's pocket, Sir Francis," Drina told him.

"I shall see that they are taken to a safe place."

When they had gone the Earl turned to look at his wife as she bathed the wound. "I thought he'd killed you," she said, her eyes brimming with tears at the very thought of all that anguish. She pressed her face into his shoulder.

"It would take more than a knock on the head to kill me," he told her gently, and then, putting his arms around her, he kissed her hair which was tumbled about her shoulders. When she raised her head he kissed her lips, lovingly at first and then with more passion.

When he drew away again she looked at him in wonderment. "Simon." She said his name softly.

"I didn't realise how much you meant to me, my love, until I found you gone. Drina, I know how you felt at the time of our marriage, but I believe you have not been unhappy. . . ."

"Unhappy! Oh, Simon, how can you think it. Just to be in the room with you has been happiness to me."

He held her very close to him. "My love," he murmured into her hair.

"I didn't expect to see you ever again," she said in an unsteady voice. "How did you find me and so soon?"

He smiled roguishly then, holding her away so he could look at her. "An impatient bridegroom will not wait for ever, my love, and I was growing more angry by the minute when you did not appear." She laughed and he traced the grimy streaks down her face with his finger. "I was just coming to look for you when Hélène came running down the corridor, waving some paper at me. She told me everything then, but it was not easy to understand her; her accent became far stronger because she was so upset, and she was almost incoherent for a while."

"He was so sure she would be too afraid to speak out."

"He went too far with her," he said grimly. "With your abduction she could take no more. Poor soul. If only she had confided in Francis at the beginning, so much unhappiness would have been avoided."

Drina frowned. "How *did* he come to be on the scene at all? I don't understand. He was in London."

"No. He had gone only as far as Cambridge because he was so worried about Hélène. He turned back, arriving just as I was about to set off. Hélène told him the story as I dressed. He cares nothing for her past, of course, and the information, such as she had, was little enough. Francis went to alert the military, but I wasn't prepared to wait. Furneaux already had too much of a start."

"It was such a dangerous thing to do, Simon. You might have been killed."

He looked grim. "As if I would consider my own safety while that fiend had you in his power. I wish I could tear him limb from limb for what he did, for what he wanted to do. Even now he is dead and you and I are safe I cannot bear to think . . ."

For four long months Drina had longed for him to look at her in just such a way. They clung to each other, kissing and hugging until the appearance of a soldier caused them to part again.

"Beggin' your pardon, my lord," the man said, averting his eyes, "I have orders to search the attic."

"Then proceed, Sergeant," the Earl told him, and for a moment or two they watched him as he poked and prodded the few sticks of furniture.

"How did you know where I had gone?" she asked.

The Earl drew his attention from the soldier and returned it to his wife once more. "Hélène was not as stupid as Furneaux thought her. She had heard mention of this place some time ago and we both thought it likely he had brought you here, especially as he indicated in his note that he was leaving for France."

On completing his task, the soldier saluted smartly and hurried back down the stairs.

"That night," the Earl said, "when I came by accident to your room . . ."

"Where *were* you going?"

"Francis suspected Hélène of being unfaithful and he charged me to watch her, only someone came down the corridor and I had to find somewhere to hide."

She laughed. "So that was it. I wish I had known."

"Do you recall my asking you to dance?"

"I shall never forget it."

"You reminded me of someone when you were so angry with your aunt and dare not speak, and it is only now that I recall who— Grandmama."

She looked horrified and he laughed. "In her youth she was the most beautiful woman of her time, full of fire and spirit. My grandfather adored her just as I adore you."

He looked at her again and she melted into his arms, but when he drew her down on to the truckle bed she said, "We must go back to Arundale Park."

"I am too ill to move. You forget I have been grievously injured."

"But our guests . . ."

"As you once said, the servants are well trained. We can be assured that they will make certain our guests have every facility."

Drina laughed and protested no more. A few moments later, when Sir Francis came up to the attic, he stared at them in astonishment, and then quickly backed down the stairs.

Historical Romance

Sparkling novels of love and conquest against the colorful background of historical England. Here are books you will savor word by word, page by spellbinding page.

☐ AFTER THE STORM—Williams	23081-3	$1.50
☐ ALTHEA—Robins	23268-9	$1.50
☐ AMETHYST LOVE—Danton	23400-2	$1.50
☐ AN AFFAIR OF THE HEART. Smith	23092-9	$1.50
☐ AUNT SOPHIE'S DIAMONDS Smith	23378-2	$1.50
☐ A BANBURY TALE—MacKeever	23174-7	$1.50
☐ CLARISSA—Arnett	22893-2	$1.50
☐ DEVIL'S BRIDE—Edwards	23176-3	$1.50
☐ ESCAPADE—Smith	23232-8	$1.50
☐ A FAMILY AFFAIR—Mellow	22967-X	$1.50
☐ THE FORTUNE SEEKER Greenlea	23301-4	$1.50
☐ THE FINE AND HANDSOME CAPTAIN—Lynch	23269-7	$1.50
☐ FIRE OPALS—Danton	23112-7	$1.50
☐ THE FORTUNATE MARRIAGE Trevor	23137-2	$1.50
☐ THE GLASS PALACE—Gibbs	23063-5	$1.50
☐ GRANBOROUGH'S FILLY Blanshard	23210-7	$1.50
☐ HARRIET—Mellows	23209-3	$1.50
☐ HORATIA—Gibbs	23175-5	$1.50

Buy them at your local bookstores or use this handy coupon for ordering:

FAWCETT BOOKS GROUP
P.O. Box C730, 524 Myrtle Ave., Pratt Station, Brooklyn, N.Y. 11205

Please send me the books I have checked above. Orders for less than 5 books must include 75¢ for the first book and 25¢ for each additional book to cover mailing and handling. I enclose $_____ in check or money order.

Name_____

Address_____

City _____ State/Zip_____

Please allow 4 to 5 weeks for delivery.

Sylvia Thorpe

Romantic tales of adventure, intrigue, and gallantry.

☐ BEGGAR ON HORSEBACK	23091-0	$1.50
☐ CAPTAIN GALLANT	23547-5	$1.75
☐ FAIR SHINE THE DAY	23229-8	$1.75
☐ A FLASH OF SCARLET	23533-5	$1.75
☐ THE CHANGING TIDE	23418-5	$1.75
☐ THE GOLDEN PANTHER	23006-6	$1.50
☐ THE RELUCTANT ADVENTURESS	23426-6	$1.50
☐ ROGUES' COVENANT	23041-4	$1.50
☐ ROMANTIC LADY	Q2910	$1.50
☐ THE SCANDALOUS LADY ROBIN	23622-6	$1.75
☐ THE SCAPEGRACE	23478-9	$1.50
☐ THE SCARLET DOMINO	23220-4	$1.50
☐ THE SILVER NIGHTINGALE	23379-9	$1.50
☐ SPRING WILL COME AGAIN	23346-4	$1.50
☐ THE SWORD AND THE SHADOW	22945-9	$1.50
☐ SWORD OF VENGEANCE	23136-4	$1.50
☐ TARRINGTON CHASE	23520-3	$1.75

Buy them at your local bookstores or use this handy coupon for ordering:

FAWCETT BOOKS GROUP
P.O. Box C730, 524 Myrtle Ave., Pratt Station, Brooklyn, N.Y. 11205

Please send me the books I have checked above. Orders for less than 5 books must include 75¢ for the first book and 25¢ for each additional book to cover mailing and handling. I enclose $_____ in check or money order.

Name_____

Address_____

City_____ State/Zip_____

Please allow 4 to 5 weeks for delivery.
